Quinn echoed Aiden's words from earlier. "I like you. You're kind of fascinating."

They hovered for a moment, drawing out the sizzling anticipation before he took her mouth, claiming her. He tasted of Scotch and smelled of heaven and temptation. A tremor ran through her body as his tongue met hers, gentler than she expected. Teasing. Inviting.

Scorching heat seared her from the inside out, melting her into his embrace. His hand slid up her neck to cup her jaw as he tilted her head back, deepening their kiss. Even though they didn't know one another, had never kissed before, he moved as if he knew her. As if he understood her.

Her hands fisted in his shirt, pulling him harder against her. His hot breath whispered across her skin as he trailed kisses along her jaw, stopping at the shell of her ear.

"Yes," she said, her breath stuttering in and out. "My answer is yes."

"I didn't ask anything." The corner of his mouth quirked up.

"Your kiss did..."

Dear Reader,

Writing each book is a unique experience, and no two books come out the same way. Sometimes the story comes to me in a flash of inspiration and others take a lot of thinking and staring off into space. Sometimes the ideas start with a plot point, a place or a theme.

And others, such as this one, start with a character.

If you read *A Dangerously Sexy Christmas*, my November 2015 Harlequin Blaze release, you may remember Quinn. She was the smart-mouthed, pink-haired tech guru who helped Max crack the case of the Noelle diamond. As soon as she appeared on the page I just knew I had to give her a happy-ever-after.

This book was so much fun to write. Since Quinn is a lover of all things video game related, I got to unleash my inner geek. I'm a child of the '80s, which I like to think of as the era of Nintendo and Super Mario Bros. So there are plenty of game references in this story!

But don't worry, if that's not your thing, there's also a dash of mystery, a hunky ex-FBI hero and plenty of sexy bits to satisfy your cravings for a steamy romance.

I really hope you enjoy Quinn and Aiden's story. You can find out what's coming next by checking out my website, stefanie-london.com, or Facebook, Facebook.com/stefanielondonauthor. I love chatting with readers, so feel free to drop me a line anytime.

With love,

Stefanie

Stefanie London

—

A Dangerously Sexy Affair

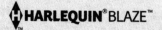

Recycling programs
for this product may
not exist in your area.

ISBN-13: 978-0-373-79894-0

A Dangerously Sexy Affair

Copyright © 2016 by Stefanie Little

Printed in U.S.A.

Stefanie London is a voracious reader who has dreamed of being an author her whole life. After sneaking several English lit subjects into her "very practical" business degree, she got a job in corporate communications. But it wasn't long before she turned to romance fiction. She recently left her hometown of Melbourne to start a new adventure in Toronto and now spends her days writing contemporary romances with humor, heat and heart.

For more information on Stefanie and her books, check out her website at stefanie-london.com or her Facebook page at Facebook.com/stefanielondonauthor.

Books by Stefanie London

Harlequin Blaze

A Dangerously Sexy Christmas

Harlequin Kiss

Breaking the Bro Code
Only the Brave Try Ballet

Harlequin Presents

The Tycoon's Stowaway

To get the inside scoop on Harlequin Blaze and its talented writers, be sure to check out BlazeAuthors.com.

All backlist available in ebook format.

Visit the Author Profile page at Harlequin.com for more titles.

To Nonno,
who taught me that nothing learned is ever wasted.

I miss you every day.

1

QUINN DELLINGER SHUFFLED closer to a potted plant and tried to pull down the hem of her dress without making it look as if she was adjusting her panties. Except pulling the dress down meant giving up any hope of a modest neckline. One wrong move could land her in wardrobe-malfunction territory, and her plans for the evening didn't include having a "nip slip" in public.

"You know, dendrophilia is kind of frowned upon." Her friend, Alana Peterson, laughed and linked her arm through Quinn's, pulling her away from the plant. "Or are you trying to take your wallflower status to the next level?"

"I'm *trying* not to show everyone what I had for lunch." Quinn pursed her lips. "This dress is obscene."

Away from the security of the curling leaves and fronds of the potted plant, Quinn was exposed to the room. Banners displaying the annual Bright Star Technology Innovation conference logo hung from the ceiling. Posters advertising the sponsors dotted the walls, and large LCD screens flashed photos from the preceding three days' worth of conference activities. But everyone in the room seemed to be more interested in talking and drinking.

"Don't be such a prude." Alana flipped her blond hair over one shoulder. "Besides, you were the one who said you wanted to get over your issues with sex. Part of that is to become comfortable with your body."

"And becoming comfortable with my body involves showing as much of it as possible?"

"Not necessarily. But you *said* you want to get back in the game, and that means you need a partner." Alana winked. "That dress looks hot. No guy in their right mind would refuse you."

"I feel like a human sausage."

"It's body con," Alana said as if it was common knowledge. "It's meant to be tight."

"I'd prefer a little less con." She rolled her eyes.

"You have an amazing body." Alana looked at her, the admiration on her face genuine and warm. "It's such a shame that you hide it all the time."

Quinn sighed. Trying to explain her complicated relationship with her body to someone who could be a Victoria's Secret model would be pointless. There wasn't anything wrong with the way she looked, not at all. But her gangly limbs, ghost-white skin and piercings weren't exactly magazine-worthy.

She hid behind pink hair dye and quirky clothes. And her "resting bitch face" may have repelled men on more than one occasion. Male attention wasn't something Quinn was ever at ease with…not when that attention could lead to humiliation.

"Besides, who says sex and networking can't go hand in hand? You might find an orgasm *and* a new job. There are some big players here—game-design studios, a few software-development companies. I'm pretty sure I saw a guy from Microsoft," Alana continued. "You're wasting your talents at that security company, and your boss has no idea what you're capable of."

She frowned. "You're right. I should have been given that promotion."

"Instead they went with someone external, who doesn't have any of your business knowledge." Alana's eyes flashed as she shook her head. "What a load of bullshit."

"Tell me about it." Quinn sighed.

Her annoyance toward Alana's pushiness—and by extension, the dress—melted away. While Alana's methods might be questionable, she'd always done her utmost to bring Quinn out of her shell.

And she was the only one Quinn could talk to about her issues with sex and her decision to conquer them. She wasn't ready to date—that required a level of trust *far* beyond her capacity—but she could reclaim her sexuality.

All she had to do was find the right guy.

"You should quit," Alana said, laying a hand on her arm and pulling her out of her thoughts. "They don't know how talented you are."

Quinn chewed on the inside of her cheek. Quitting sounded so simple when Alana said it in that airy way of hers, but that would mean going through the interview process again…and if there was one thing she sucked at, it was interviews. And even if she got a new job, she'd have to start working with a different team and go through that epic awkwardness of being the "new girl" all over again.

It wasn't only that. She *liked* working at Cobalt &

Dane. She admired her manager and appreciated all that they achieved as a company. She didn't intend to quit—she simply had to prove they'd made a mistake by not promoting her. Being part of the technology security division at Cobalt & Dane Security was her dream, and after three years working as an IT support officer, she knew that she wanted more out of her career. That she was *capable* of more.

"I'm getting that job," Quinn said through gritted teeth. "The new guy is a temporary hurdle."

Alana raised a brow. "A temporary hurdle?"

"Yep. I'm going to make it my mission to prove to my boss that I'm *exactly* the person he needs."

"You've already proven it, but they haven't been paying attention." Alana frowned, her blue eyes narrowing.

"Ease up, Mama Bear. I'm happy to show them what I'm made of."

The two girls stood to the side of the room and watched the crowd. It was an eclectic mix of people: men in suits and others in jeans, old and young, a wonderful melting pot of nationalities and cultures.

But almost *all* men.

As a self-professed tech-head and an avid gamer, Quinn was used to being a minority. She and Alana had bonded immediately in high school because they were often the only two girls in their IT class. They'd both gone on to study technology at college and had entered the industry still feeling as if they didn't quite belong.

Alana had taken it on the chin and ended up using her model looks to get ahead. She figured if men were going to objectify her then she'd use it to her advantage. Quinn, on the other hand, was the typical introvert. She worked better with small groups, had a few close friends she held dear and kept everyone else at arm's length.

"If you keep pulling on that dress, you're going to ruin the hem," Alana admonished. "I'll make you pay for it."

"And I'll challenge you to 'Mortal Kombat,' winner takes all," Quinn pointed out.

"I wouldn't be stupid enough to fall for that twice." Alana's glossy lips lifted into a rueful smile. "Talk about an embarrassing defeat."

"Less than twenty seconds, if my memory serves me correctly."

"I still maintain you cheated."

Quinn laughed. "Whatever helps you sleep at night."

The room buzzed around them, music mixing with conversation and the sound of laughter. Waiters wove through the crowds carrying silver trays filled with champagne, wine and beer. Quinn hadn't been to a cocktail party before, and she was surprised that they weren't actually serving cocktails. Not that she really gravitated to drinks with little umbrellas in them, but still…

"Do you actually know anyone here?" Quinn asked, accepting a glass of red wine from a passing waiter. She sipped and tried not to cringe at the taste; this was so *not* her style.

"Only the guy who got us added to the list. I recognize a few people. That guy—" Alana pointed to an older man in a gray suit "—he's the CEO of Strikevision. I'm pretty sure I saw one of the guys from Popstar Games here, as well."

Quinn nodded. She wasn't impressed by celebrities or reality TV stars, but put the man responsible for

"Saints Row" in front of her and she'd fangirl like a sixteen-year-old at a Justin Bieber concert.

"So why are *you* here? I don't buy that it's just to be my winglady."

"I'm working on a story," Alana admitted.

"You lured me here under false pretenses?" Quinn tugged at the hem of her dress again. *"And* you make me wear this hideously uncomfortable thing. Not cool at all."

"It's for a good cause. I got a sneak peek at Third Planet Studios' plans for the next Galactic Warrior game. It's the same old bullshit again—strong men saving weak little damsels in distress. I've been trying to get an interview with one of the designers to ask why they never have any female protagonists in their games."

"Let me guess, he doesn't want to have a bar of your feminist outrage." Quinn shook her head. "And you want to hang them out to dry."

"It's my job."

Alana ran one of the most prominent gaming news sites on the internet. She'd made a small fortune creating a space for female gamers to convene without judgment or objectification. Despite being called every horrible name under the sun—not to mention constantly battling vitriolic misogyny on every social media platform—Alana was determined to change the gaming industry. Quinn often contributed game reviews and blog posts in her spare time, happy to do anything to support her friend's business since the issue was close to her heart, too.

"When I have a daughter, I want her to be able to play video games that empower her." Alana stared out into the crowd, her face set into a mask of determination. "I don't want her to be treated like a second-class citizen when she goes to a gaming convention."

"Amen, sister."

Alana paused, sipping on her champagne. "Is it so bad that I wanted you here for moral support?"

"You could have told me. Besides, I'm not going to be much help. You know you're the outgoing, pretty one, and I'm the quiet, smart one." She tried to keep a straight face but it was near impossible. If they weren't at a professional event, Alana would have socked her in the arm.

"Aside from the fact that we're *both* smart, it makes me sad that you undervalue yourself."

"Please don't get all Dr. Phil on me," she groaned. "I wore the goddamn dress. You don't get any other freebies tonight."

"I repeat—that dress makes you look hot. I hope you get some." Alana winked. "Sex is natural and healthy. You deserve to feel good about it again."

"It's not that easy." She swirled her wineglass slowly and watched as the red wine clung to the edges. "What if I can't find a guy who's attracted to me?"

"Then the world is full of fucking morons and we may as well give up hope."

"I love it when you swear. It's like a Care Bear giving someone the finger."

Alana's laughter stopped short as her eyes locked onto someone across the room. Target acquired.

"Aha! A Third Planet designer. I'm going to charm him into talking to me." She squeezed Quinn's shoulder. "Then I'm going to take him down."

Alana walked away, and Quinn stifled a laugh as several men almost gave themselves whiplash trying to keep their eyes on her. She could hardly blame them; Alana was perfect.

All. The. Damn. Time.

At one point it had intimidated Quinn; now it only baffled her. Maybe her friend wasn't human...

Quinn backed up until something brushed against her leg, making her jump. The tree.

"It's you and me, old friend," she said, positive she looked like a nutcase for talking to a plant. "Want to get drunk?"

AIDEN ODELL EXCUSED himself from a conversation that was quickly heading south. Tinder hookups weren't something he cared about. Frankly, he didn't need an app to help him in that area of his life.

Besides, tonight was all about work. Tomorrow would be his first official day at Cobalt & Dane Security and he'd already been assigned a case. The head of Third Planet Studios—an up-and-coming game design company—was about to launch a new project, which up until recently had been kept quiet. But someone was leaking details.

He'd called in a favor to get access to the cocktail party in the hopes of picking up information. And he'd also booked a room at the hotel in case he needed to work into the night.

This was Aiden's chance to show people what he was made of. Not only that, his best friend—the Dane in Cobalt & Dane—had been asking him to join his team for a year. It would be a turning point for Aiden, a fresh start. He'd be able to work at a place where his expertise was valued. No more handouts because of who his father was; no more free passes or special treatment.

And he was determined to hit the ground running. Success would be his, no matter what. Even if it meant giving up part of his weekend to do optional recon.

However, he'd picked up nothing but flimsy rumors all night. Definitely nothing that hinted at who was involved. Now, several hours later, he was tired of banal conversation and dead ends. The king-size bed in his hotel room called to him. It was late and he *should* get a good night's sleep.

Aiden shrugged off the temptation. The only lead he had was a leggy blonde by the name of Alana Peterson, who apparently had some kind of grudge against the company. But his attempt to engage her in conversation had resulted in his being turned down flatter than a pancake.

A flash of color caught his attention. A woman stood next to a potted plant, her lithe figure encased in a little black dress that was hot enough to melt brain cells. But it was her hair that captivated him. It tumbled down to her waist, dark brown at the top and hot-pink through the lengths. She had a nose piercing and five earrings in one ear. He couldn't help but linger; she was sex on a stick.

Plus, he'd seen her talking to Alana Peterson earlier. Were they friends? Or simply two women gravitating toward one another in a sea of men?

The woman turned to the potted plant, her lips moving. Was she talking to a *tree*?

A laugh bubbled up in his throat. She was definitely more appealing than a bunch of geeky men whining about online dating…even if she did appear to be talking to an inanimate object.

"What does your friend think of the party?" he asked, coming up beside her.

She jumped. "Excuse me?"

"Your friend." He inclined his head toward the tree. "You were talking to him, weren't you?"

"Her," the woman corrected, her face totally neutral. "This is Leafina."

"Nice to meet you, Leafina." He grabbed a frond, shaking it up and down. "And you are?"

"Not a tree." The corner of her lip twitched as she accepted his proffered hand.

Damn, she was gorgeous. Quirky, a little awkward, but sexy as all get-out.

"I'm Aiden, also not a tree. I'm not much of a party-goer, either." Something warned him being overconfident wouldn't work with her—hopefully, he'd read her right.

Her face softened. "Me, neither. Are you here by yourself?"

"Yeah, but this is a work thing." He flagged down a passing waiter and grabbed a glass of red wine. "I'd rather be home, to tell you the truth."

She made an adorable snorting noise, bobbing her head in agreement. "I got dragged here by a friend."

"So you're not a tech-head?"

"Oh, I am, but I do that on my own time."

He sipped his drink. "Who's your friend? I might know them."

"Alana Peterson. She's a tech reporter."

Bingo. Not only were they friends, but they'd come here together. If Alana was involved in the leak, this woman might have heard about it.

"I'm familiar with the name, but I don't think I've met her."

"You would remember if you had." A genuine smile tugged at her lips. "She's quite a force."

"Is she working on a story?"

"Yeah. She's always fighting for better representation of women in the gaming industry," the woman said, her voice tinted with pride. "She wants one of the game companies to commit to having a female lead in their games. Or at the very least she wants to find out why they haven't had one to date."

Ah, so that must be the grudge he'd heard about. "That game company wouldn't happen to be Third Planet Studios, would it?"

She blinked. "How did you know that?"

"People talk. Her opinions have caused a stir, and not too many guys here seem to care about feminism."

"Color me shocked." Quinn rolled her eyes. "That only proves why we need people like Alana asking questions."

"You're absolutely right." He breathed a sigh of relief.

He could recognize a lie when he heard one—he knew how to detect the sound of it, how to look for the telltale facial movements and tics. And how to do all of that without giving a thing away himself.

Thankfully, there was nothing but honesty in this enigmatic woman's responses.

Which meant he could keep talking to her without the weight of suspicion hanging over them.

"Who do you work for?" she asked.

"Ricochet Studios," he said, keeping to his script.

The plan was to tell people he was a game designer, some low-level minion at a big company where no one would be likely to call him out on the lie. He had enough knowledge to have a basic discussion about game design, and he was adept at manipulating conversation should anyone get close to sniffing him out.

His experience working for the FBI had equipped him to skate the truth with ease, not that he took any pleasure in it. But his job came first.

"The company who made 'Slayer's Faith'?" Her pink lips parted. "You worked on that game?"

The reverence in her voice was a huge boost to his ego, which was stupid since it meant nothing. "You play?"

"I clocked over a hundred hours on it. You don't make it easy to get the platinum trophy." She folded her arms, the action plumping up her breasts so that they pressed together in the deep V of the dress's neckline. "It wasn't quite as bad as finding all the pigeons in 'GTA Four,' mind you."

A hot girl who knew her games? Heaven must have been smiling down on him. "Ah, you're a completionist."

"All the best gamers are."

He took a slow sip of his wine. "What's your favorite game?"

"That's like asking me to pick a favorite limb." Her dark brows creased.

"Chicken." He laughed when she narrowed her gaze at him.

The diamond in her nose winked in the light and she tapped a finger to her cheek. The chipped black polish on her fingernails seemed at odds with the hotter-than-sin dress and sexy heels. But he enjoyed the combo; a little bit of contradiction made things more exciting…

like there were secrets to be uncovered. A real person under the gloss.

"'Slayer's Faith,'" she said, nodding as if convincing herself. "Followed closely by 'Mario Kart.'"

"What about Leafina? What does she play?" He looked at the potted plant again and a laugh burst from the pink-haired woman's lips.

"Can I tell you a secret?" she said, her hazel eyes glinting.

"Sure."

She leaned in close to his ear and cupped a hand around her mouth. "Leafina is kind of boring."

Her hot breath on his neck flipped an "on" switch deep inside him and filled his whole body with energy. Damn.

He turned toward her, his nose inches from her cheek. "What did you say your name was?"

He realized then that she had hardly any makeup on. Her lashes were dark but not artificial, leaving the unusual green and gold flecks in her eyes to stand out on their own. Her pupils were wide, black.

A delicate blush spread out across her cheeks. "You can call me Pink."

"Oh, it's like that, is it?" He took a step closer until the space between them shrank to mere inches. "You're playing hard to get."

"I'm worth it."

He didn't doubt her for a second.

2

QUINN SIPPED HER WINE, the need for a little Dutch courage outweighing her dislike of the taste. The man in front of her was hot with a capital *H*—curly black hair, a sharp jaw and blue eyes that burned right through her...not to mention a pair of soft jeans that molded to his thighs like a dream—and she was *flirting* with him.

She didn't flirt. Ever.

"I bet you're a whiz at 'Super Mario,'" Aiden said.

"What makes you say that?" She shifted on the high heels Alana had lent her, wishing that she was wearing something more comfortable.

Having a gorgeous guy stand so close to her was making her body haywire enough; she didn't need to compound the effect with precariously tall heels. All that talk of sex and orgasms with Alana had her wound up tighter than a coil. Could this guy be the one to help her get back in the proverbial game?

She didn't know him from a bar of soap...which was kind of the point. One-night stands didn't end in betrayal because there were no expectations for tomorrow.

"You've got good gamer hands," he said.

"Really?" She swallowed, curling her fingers into a fist to hide the chipped polish that she hadn't had time to remove.

"Yeah, I can tell. Those are magic hands."

She laughed and shook her head, hoping her face didn't convey the electric thrill he'd given her. How was it possible for her to be so attracted to him so quickly? In the past it had taken her months of chatting to someone online before she would agree to meet and, even then, it would take several dates before she'd be comfortable enough to even fool around. Until she'd dated her ex…

She shuddered. No man had gotten close to her since. But two years had passed; she'd recovered. Moved on. And her libido had definitely returned.

"So tell me, Pink. What do you do for a living?"

Quinn took a swallow of her wine, stalling. She didn't want to admit she was a lowly IT support officer, especially not when his job was so exciting. But she didn't want to lie and say she was a tech-security expert, either, because that job wasn't hers…yet.

"I, uh…" She swirled the wine in her glass. "I'm actually trying to figure out where I'm going."

"That's sufficiently vague," Aiden said, laughing. "I get it. You don't have any reason to trust me."

"Don't take it personally. I don't trust Leafina, either," she quipped.

"I'm going to be bold." He drained the remainder of his wine and handed the glass off to a passing waiter. "I like you, Pink. You're kind of fascinating."

"Kind of?" Heat crawled up her cheeks as she looked out at the crowd, her eyes searching for Alana. She wanted to signal to her friend that she was about to make good on her plan.

"Yeah. You're also kind of hot." His words smoothed over her like a caress. "Okay, that's a total lie. You're *insanely* hot."

"And you're *kind of* smooth." Her voice came out far steadier than she'd expected. "I bet that works on a lot of girls."

"Is that your way of saying it's not going to work on you?"

The last third of her wine mocked her. She brought the glass to her lips and finished it in one smooth gulp. "I didn't say that."

"You want me to work for it?"

"Damn straight."

His arm snaked around her waist, drawing her closer. "That I can do. How about I take you for a proper drink?"

Could she really do it? Part of her resisted the idea of going for a drink with a man she didn't know, but her attraction to Aiden sizzled, and no warning bells had sounded thus far.

"I'm a red belt in Tae Kwon Do." She tilted her head up to him. "And I know a lot of scary people."

"Pink, I'm not going to do anything that you don't want me to do. If at any point you decide to call it a night, I will organize a cab and see that you get home safely." His breath was warm against her neck as he lowered his head. The scent of aftershave and wine mingled in her nostrils. "If you don't want to leave... I'm more than happy to oblige there, too."

A delicious shiver ran up the length of her spine. "I'll take you up on that drink."

"Do you need to tell Alana where we're going?"

"I'll text her."

Aiden's hand found the small of her back as he escorted her out of the cocktail party and into the lobby of the hotel. Alana was nowhere to be seen. Her friend would understand, but she texted her anyway.

"Tell her my name is Aiden Odell, room two-thirty-two," he said. "We'll be having a drink in the Lion Lounge if she wants to come find you."

Typing with her thumbs, Quinn sent the details through to Alana. Slipping the phone into her bag, she swallowed down any reservations and allowed Aiden to guide her toward the dimly lit bar on the other side of the hotel lobby.

Two hours later they were sitting on a leather sofa, surrounded by soft lighting designed for intimacy. They were also several Scotches down and in midargument about who was a more avid gamer.

"I got my first console at six years old," Quinn said, gesturing with her glass, the last bit of liquid swishing precariously up the side. "I've kept every single one since then."

"Console collecting does not make you a master gamer." Aiden shook his head, his dark curls looking slightly wild and out of control.

Her fingers ached to run through them, to tug them until his head was right where she wanted it. "If you had one in your hotel room, I would prove to you right now that I could kick your ass in *any* game."

"That's a bold statement, Pink." He leaned forward and braced his forearms on his thighs, nursing a crystal tumbler in both hands. "But it's complete crap."

"It is not!" She pursed her lips and tried to be mad.

But truth was, she loved the banter and the fact that he challenged her. Most male gamers wouldn't even bother; they'd assume she wasn't their equal and move on.

"It is." He rolled the glass between his hands, warming the last of his drink. "Because if I took you up to my room, the only thing you'd be playing would be me."

Her sex clenched and she pressed her thighs together, failing to dull the throbbing. "How can you be certain I'm not going to thank you for the drinks and then leave?"

"I can't." He grinned, a wicked glint lighting up his vibrant eyes. "But if you're half as attracted to me as I am to you…well, then it's going to be fun."

"You don't know anything about me."

He leaned back in his seat, finished off his drink and set it down on the mirror-finish table in front of them. "So fill me in. You don't have to tell me your name or what you do. Or anything serious."

"A random fact, then?"

"Yeah, something you think other people wouldn't care about." He rolled up the sleeves of his cotton shirt, exposing arms smattered with dark hair.

His denim-clad thigh sat inches from hers, and heat pulsed between them. Over the past couple of hours, she'd kept her space and he hadn't pushed, hadn't tried to make a direct move. But his words and actions were heavy with intent, each naughty suggestion pushing her further and further toward deciding to go upstairs with him.

"I'm an only child," she said, figuring that such a benign detail was probably safe to share. "And I prefer it that way."

"You never wanted a brother or a sister?"

"I don't like sharing my toys." She laughed. "I do things my way, on *my* terms."

"Yeah, I got that impression." His eye raked over her. "I have a brother *and* a sister."

The darkness in his tone made her pause, but the friendly smile sprang back into place. "So how do you know Alana? Are you a tech reporter, too?"

She shook her head. "We went to school together. When she started her site, I offered to review games for her."

"I bet she gets a lot of inside information."

"Yeah, she does. Lots of companies send her pre-release stuff, and she's *always* getting invited to parties like this." Quinn smirked. "Then she drags me along and bails when a story comes up."

Aiden paused and took a swig of his Scotch. "I'm surprised she's not looking into the game engine Third Planet is building. There's been a lot of buzz about that lately."

Game engine? "I haven't heard anything about that."

"Really?" He cocked his head. "Apparently, it's going to revolutionize the way games are designed."

"I guess she would be interested in that."

A dimple formed in his cheek as he smiled. "Okay, that's enough nerd talk from me."

"Don't stop on my account." She held up a hand and laughed. "I'm all for nerd talk."

"What if I want to talk about you?" His eyes raked over her, hot and steady, lighting a path from her cheeks straight down to her sex.

"I don't really enjoy talking about myself. Call it a lesson learned."

His lips pressed into a line. "Sounds like you've got a bad story there."

Was he genuinely concerned? Probably not. After all, they didn't really know each other. She hadn't told him her real name, where she worked or lived…but those were her rules. A one-night stand would be fine because she could call it quits when *she* wanted, and Aiden couldn't come after her if he didn't have her name.

"I'm a big girl. I can look after myself." She squared her shoulders. "So, two siblings, huh?"

"Yeah, but I'm not good at sharing, either."

"Maybe we won't be compatible, then," she said with mock seriousness. "We both hate sharing. We're both competitive."

"I've always found competition to be a healthy thing." The words came out rough, low.

"Even where sex is concerned?" She bit her lip.

"*Especially* where sex is concerned." His arms slid along the back of the sofa, and Quinn scooted closer to him until their knees were touching.

"I'm going to be bold," she said, echoing his words from earlier. "I like you. You're kind of fascinating."

"Kind of?" he asked as his head dipped, his lips inches from hers.

"Yeah, kind of."

They both hovered for a moment, drawing out the sizzling anticipation before he slanted his mouth over hers, claiming her. He tasted of Scotch and smelled of heaven and temptation. A tremor ran through her body as his tongue met hers, gentler than she expected. Teasing. Inviting.

Scorching heat seared her from the inside out, melting her into his embrace. His hand slid up her neck to cup her jaw. Then he tilted her head back, deepening their kiss. Even though they'd never kissed before, he moved as if he knew her. As if he understood her.

Her hands fisted in his shirt, pulling him harder against her. His hot breath whispered across her skin as he trailed kisses along her jaw, stopping at the shell of her ear.

"Yes," she said, her breath stuttering in and out. "My answer is yes."

"I didn't ask anything." The corner of his mouth quirked.

"Your kiss did." She released his shirt and stood, holding her hand out to him.

AIDEN HELD PINK close to his body as they walked through the hotel lobby and into the bay of elevators. She interlaced her fingers with his, her small hand gripping him tightly. He couldn't remember the last time any kiss had made him feel this much anticipation.

Guilt churned in his gut that he hadn't been completely honest with her. He didn't have a problem with lying on the job—it was often a requirement, in fact—but this *wasn't* work. And she wasn't an asset or a suspect. Judging by the blank stare she'd given him when he'd asked about the gaming engine, she didn't know anything. So taking her up to his room was purely personal, and he wanted to make that clear.

The elevator dinged and they filed in behind two other couples. Keeping himself from touching her was torture, especially when Pink leaned back against him, her sweet behind fitting directly against his crotch.

Stifling a groan, he thrust his hips slightly to press into her.

She looked over her shoulder, a sly smile on her lips. "Competitive *and* impatient."

"I never said I was perfect."

Mercifully, the elevator stopped and they were first out. Laughter filtered into the hallway from one of the rooms, mixing with the soothing classical music playing through the hotel speakers. The whole scene was calm and in complete contradiction to the arousal raging inside him.

"Hey, there's something I should tell you," he said as they walked hand in hand down the corridor toward his hotel room.

"You're not married, are you?" Their steps were muffled by the plush carpeting. "Or a serial killer?"

"No," he said with a laugh. "But I'm—"

"I don't want to know." They stopped outside his hotel room door and she held up a hand. "So long as you're not cheating on anyone by being with me and you have no intention of hurting me, I don't care about the rest."

He hesitated and uncertainty flickered in her eyes. "We're fine on both counts. You have my word."

"Good. Because we're both aware what this is, and we don't need to be coy about it." Her voice wavered but he wasn't about to call her out on it. "It's sex. I don't need any more detail than that."

As much as he would have preferred to come clean there and then, she'd made her case. If she only wanted sex, then that was fine by him. More than fine, in fact.

"Fair enough." He swiped the key card and pushed open the door.

It wasn't a fancy suite—playing the role of a lowly tech employee meant skipping on the extravagant hotel room—but the large king-size bed would be more than enough. Not to mention the double shower that had been a pleasant surprise when he'd checked in.

He imagined Pink with water streaming over her naked body, and the picture was enough to make whatever blood was left in his head rush south. His cock strained painfully against his fly.

"We can still stop at any time if you're not comfortable," he said as she surveyed the room, an unreadable expression on her face.

As desperate as he was to touch her, he needed to hear her say she was in.

"I'm comfortable." She nodded, stepping toward him. A shy smile played on her lips. "But I'd be more comfortable if you got me out of this dress."

"I can definitely help with that." He grabbed her hand and planted a soft kiss on her lips before turning her around. A gold zipper ran from between her shoulder blades to the sweet curve above her ass. She reached around to sweep her long hair over one shoulder, exposing the delicate line of her neck. His lips gravitated to the spot, as if pulled by a magnetic force. The scent of her creamy skin—soapy and clean—teased him as his hands smoothed down the lengths of her arms.

A shudder ran through her and goose bumps rippled across her skin as he gently scraped his teeth along her shoulder. He tugged on her zipper, drawing it down with deliberate slowness. One didn't rush a decadent dessert; you savored each and every bite.

And that was exactly what he intended to do with Pink.

The V of bare skin deepened, and soon it was obvious that she wasn't wearing a bra. Lord help him, this woman was hot enough to start a wildfire.

"You still breathing back there?" she asked, her tone dancing with laughter.

"Just admiring the view." He pushed the dress from her body and it slid to the floor.

She stepped out of the puddle of fabric, kicking it to the side. Bright pink panties barely covered the gentle curves of her ass and hips.

"Are those ninjas on your underwear?" he asked, spinning her around.

"They might be." She ran her palms up the front of his chest until they curled over his shoulders, pressing him down. "Perhaps you should take a closer inspection."

He kissed his way down her stomach until he was on his knees, his lips at the waistband of her panties. "Hmm, they *do* appear to have ninjas on them. You know what this means, right?"

Her nails dragged against his scalp as she threaded her fingers through his hair. "What?"

"They're likely to disappear any second." Hooking a finger under the elastic band, he tugged the fabric down.

Pink-colored cotton pooled at her feet, the bright shade a sharp contrast to the high gloss of her black leather pumps. Holy. Hell.

He planted a palm on her thigh to keep her steady as she stepped out of the underwear and then the heels. "See, gone."

"Like magic." Her voice was rough and husky, the sound fanning his desire.

He felt pretty damn magical indeed. Taking a gorgeous woman to bed was exactly the antidote he needed for the recent negativity in his life. He'd pour all that pent-up frustration and tension into pleasuring Pink out of her ever-loving mind. If she didn't scream his name until her voice gave out, then he would consider the night a failure.

"You look so serious," she said, running her fingers through his hair.

He kissed her hip then smoothed his palm up the inside of her thigh as if he could use his touch to commit her dimensions to memory. Everything about her was delicate, and yet she had an inner strength and conviction that he found utterly irresistible. This was a woman who did things on her own terms.

"That's because I'm seriously hot for you." He pressed his lips to her sex in a gentle kiss—a prelude to what he intended to do next.

She gasped and tightened her grip on his hair, flipping on every damn switch in his body. His cock twitched in his pants.

"Hmm…" The sound washed over him from above. "Really?"

Her tone might have been playful, but he was serious as all hell. "Absolutely."

He ran his tongue up the seam of her sex, parting her folds until he found the swollen bud of her clit. Gripping her thigh with one hand, he used his thumb to part her, giving him the access he wanted.

"Oh, Aiden."

Hearing his name drove him on. He lapped at her with his tongue, insistent, demanding.

All sense of restraint and slow enjoyment flew out the window as he relentlessly pursued her orgasm.

Drawing her clit between his lips, he flicked it with his tongue and tremors racked her body.

"I can't... I can't..."

"Yes." He punctuated his words with hot kisses. "You. Can."

Her thighs trembled in his grasp, her hips tilting forward as she rubbed herself shamelessly against his mouth.

"I'm close," she gasped.

He parted her legs and touched his fingers to her sex, sliding one digit slowly inside. A shudder ran through her body, and a string of incoherent words dissolved into a moan as she tipped over the edge, her sex pulsing against his lips.

Her cries bounced off the hotel room walls and she sagged forward, her knees hitting his chest. He gathered her up in his arms and carried her to the bed.

A sigh escaped her lips as she lolled her head back against his biceps, her eyes fluttering. "If you'd told me you could do *that* with your mouth, I might not have made you work so hard to get me up here."

"I wasn't going to bribe you with orgasms."

"You should have." A blissful smile pulled at her lips. "We wasted two hours drinking."

"How about we make up for it now?" he suggested, one knee sinking into the mattress as he lowered her to the bed.

"I don't have time for your rhetorical questions." A laugh rumbled in her throat and she reached up, grabbing him by the shirt and pulling him down roughly. "Come here."

3

QUINN CLOSED HER eyes as Aiden came down over her, his weight pressing her into the soft mattress. It was like being trapped between a fluffy cloud and a god. A sex god, if that orgasm was anything to go on.

Her body hummed, hovering in some crazy limbo between roaring hunger and total satisfaction. It had been a while since she'd come that hard, and his mouth was so, so, *so* much better than her trusty vibrator.

Cupping the back of her head, he slid his tongue across her lips, opening her. Allowing her to taste herself.

She moaned into him and heat fanned out across her chest as he moved down her body. There was something graceful about his movement, something sleek and elegant and primal. He captured a nipple with his lips and sucked. Hard.

"Oh." Words escaped her as he laved her breast, tugging, licking, worshipping.

"What do you want, Pink?"

"I want… Ahhhhh."

Colors danced behind her closed eyelids as he pushed

his hips against hers, his length rubbing over her still-sensitive sex. Denim rasped over her soft skin, the steely hardness making her pulse race.

"Say it," he growled against her breast, his teeth working her into a frenzy. "Tell me."

"I want you inside me," she gasped.

"No."

Her head snapped up, eyes unblinking. If she didn't have him now, she might explode… At the very least she'd wear her vibrator out trying to make up for not having him. "What do you mean?"

"I still don't know your name." He released his grip, bringing his head up to lock that electric gaze straight on her.

"I'm Pink," she stammered, the haze of excitement fogging her mind.

"Your *real* name." A dark curl fell over his forehead and he brushed it aside.

"What does it matter?" She pushed herself up and reached for the top button of his shirt. "It won't change how incredible this is going to be."

"I remember the name of every girl I've ever slept with, and if this is going to be as incredible as I think it will be…" He paused.

Flattening her palms against his chest, she pushed him back until he sat on his heels. "Yes?"

"I want to know what name to moan in your ear when I'm inside you."

Quinn's hands trembled as she undid the buttons on his shirt. Dark hair dusted his chest, tapering to a V down the hard plane of his stomach and dipping below the waistband of his jeans.

She sucked in a breath and tried to steady herself.

She *never* lost her wits, ever. Aiden, however, was doing crazy things to her. Crazy, astoundingly pleasurable things.

"It's Quinn," she said, her hands working at the button on his fly.

He placed his hand over hers, warm and reassuring. "Quinn."

"Are you going to tell me it's a beautiful name?" she quipped, sarcasm her natural and comfortable shield.

"I doubt saying the expected thing would win me any favors with you." He moved her hand away and stood, dragging the zipper on his fly down.

"It wouldn't."

As he stripped himself of his jeans and briefs, Quinn couldn't help but stare. She knew more than anyone that computer geeks didn't always fit into the stereotypes or clichés. But she hadn't expected Aiden to be so...powerful.

Muscular thighs met trim hips, the hard jut of his cock making her blood fizz. God, she wanted him like nothing else.

"Wow," she whispered.

His eyes crinkled as he laughed. "Thanks for the ego boost."

Heat flared through her, filling her neck and cheeks. "I mean...uh..."

"You can stop at *wow*." He brushed the hair from her face. "I'm definitely okay with that."

She touched her fingers to the tip of him, hesitating before wrapping them around his shaft. He made a guttural noise at the back of his throat that urged her on. She slid her hand up and down, stroking him.

"Quinn," he moaned and pushed his hips forward into her grip. "That's so damn good."

Emboldened by his praise, she parted her lips and leaned forward, drawing him into her mouth. The head of his cock slid along her tongue and she tasted a faint saltiness. Eyes closed, she bobbed her head down as far as she could go.

At the same time she ran her hand up and down his thigh, his hairs tickling her palm. The scent of earthy maleness danced in her nose.

"That's enough." His voice came out strangled. Edgy.

She eased him out of her mouth and swirled her tongue over the tip of him. "What if I'm not ready to stop?"

He grunted, sweeping the hair over her shoulder and easing her back. "I'm not going to last more than five seconds if you keep that up."

"You're not the only one who's skilled with their mouth."

"Damn straight." He scooped up his jeans and dug a foil packet from his wallet, then tore it open in one smooth motion and rolled the condom down on himself.

His arm slid around her waist and he eased them down to the bed, his knees nudging her thighs apart. Warmth enveloped her as he pressed her into the mattress, the weight of him deliciously comforting. His lips found the crook of her collarbone, and she looped her arms around his neck.

"You're so beautiful." He planted a hot, openmouthed kiss on her lips.

"I thought you weren't going to say what was expected," she murmured, tugging on his lower lip with her teeth.

His cock pressed at her entrance, rubbing against her in a way that made her whole body ache with desperation. "I'm serious. You're absolutely incredible and unique."

She buried her face against his neck, unsure of how to react to the compliment. It was one thing for her to joke about herself, but another thing entirely for him to mean it. Instead of responding, she sucked on his skin, rolling her hips up against his. Showing him what she wanted instead of telling him.

He entered her in one fluid movement, the shock of his thickness pushing all the air from her lungs. A brief flash of pain gave way to liquid heat, honeyed and soothing and all-encompassing.

"God, Quinn." He gasped against her hair. "You're so tight. So perfect."

"Take me. Please."

And he did. With abandon.

Her nails dug into his back as he pumped into her, his hips knocking against hers, each stroke brushing her sex and pushing her closer to the peak. She grabbed his face in her hands and forced his mouth down to hers, meeting him thrust for thrust.

"So good," he murmured, his eyes squeezed shut. "Oh, Quinn. Christ!"

An orgasm crashed into her as he plunged deep, his body trembling against hers. Their names mixed together, passed between each other's lips as they fell into shared oblivion.

QUINN'S EYELIDS FLUTTERED OPEN. She tried to push the hair from her face and realized she couldn't move. Not

an inch. She hadn't had that much to drink at the party...
had she?

The bed shifted and something hard pressed against
her ass, an arm tightening around her. Then it came
flooding back: talking to Aiden, drinks at the bar followed by a string of life-changing orgasms.

Shit.

She'd done it...she'd actually had sex without freak-
ing out.

And she'd slept through the night. When had *that*
happened last? Normally, it would take an hour or two
of "Slayer's Faith" before she could even contemplate
crawling into bed, and then she'd stick her earbuds in,
tossing fitfully to some bullshit relaxation track until
sleep finally claimed her. Temporarily, anyway.

The last time she'd slept all the way through without
waking was... She couldn't remember.

His arm was a deadweight over her midsection. His
thighs lined hers and his crotch cradled her ass. Apparently, what they did last night hadn't worn him out...not
if the steel rod digging into her was anything to go on.

Easing herself out of Aiden's grip, she shuffled to the
edge of the bed and grabbed her phone. Three missed
calls from Alana and a handful of texts. Oh, and it was
6:00 a.m.

Double shit!

She had to get across the bridge to her Brooklyn
apartment so she could change for work. A subway
ride of shame wasn't exactly appealing, but a cab might
not be quick enough. Biting down on her lip, her mind
spun, searching for a solution.

Moving as gingerly as possible, she swung her legs
out of the bed and stood. There was no time for awk-

ward morning-after conversation. Besides, she'd been very clear what she'd wanted from him.

Aiden's resting form could have been used for a mattress commercial; the hint of a smile on his lips and the messy splay of his dark curls made him look angelic.

But there sure as hell hadn't been anything angelic about last night.

Quinn pressed the heel of her hand to the throbbing spot between her eyes. She needed to get out. Now.

Tiptoeing across the room, she gathered her panties and her dress and slipped both on as stealthily as she could. Alana's patent leather stilettos gleamed beside the bed, still standing upright from when she'd discarded them last night. Heat surged through her as she remembered exactly what had happened after she'd shed them, her knees wobbling at the memory.

Holding the heels in one hand and her purse in the other, she glanced at Aiden. He mumbled in his sleep, rolling onto his back. The sheet came up over his hips, outlining an impressive erection. Swallowing, she let her eyes linger for a moment before sneaking for the door.

Part of her wanted to scribble down her number and leave it for him to find, but a relationship wasn't in her plan. She had a promotion to chase and a personal life to sort out before she inflicted her problems on someone else...and her gut told her that seeing Aiden again would be like trying to take drugs without getting addicted.

You both agreed, no strings. You don't owe him anything.

Quinn opened the hotel room door just enough to squeeze through, and she held her breath as it closed behind her.

As she walked barefoot to the elevator, her phone buzzed, Alana's face flashing on the screen.

"Hello?"

"You slept with someone?" Alana's high-pitched squeal ricocheted in Quinn's head, making her flinch.

"Jesus, Alana. Can you *not* scream?" She shook her head, trying to clear the ringing in her ears. "And you say that with such amazement. I wasn't a virgin, you know."

She stopped at the elevator and jabbed the call button repeatedly, bouncing on the balls of her feet as she waited. Hopefully, the early hour would mean she wouldn't have to walk past many people in a dress that was barely decent for a cocktail party, let alone breakfast.

"I know but it's exciting. You're getting past your…"

"Mental deformities?"

Pause. "Trust concerns."

Quinn rolled her eyes. "Yeah, that sounds a whole lot better."

"So who is he?"

"A designer for Ricochet Studios." Quinn drew her bottom lip between her teeth. "Kind of cool that I slept with a guy who worked on 'Slayer's Faith.'"

Alana snorted. "I could make so many jokes right now."

"Don't. And, before you ask, no, I'm *not* going to see him again."

Alana sighed. "I get it. Baby steps. Where are you, anyway?"

"I'm still at the hotel."

"Me, too." A sly laugh came through the line. "You're not the only dirty birdie here. I'll meet you downstairs in a few minutes and then we can head to my place."

Alana's was only a short walk away. She could shower and change and be at the office in forty-five minutes tops. "Any chance I can borrow something to wear to work?"

"Of course."

Quinn stepped into the elevator and pressed the button for the lobby. Mercifully, the doors closed and no one else had joined her. "See you in a minute."

Dropping the phone into her bag, she sagged against the elevator. Drained. Her whole body thrummed with satisfaction but a monster coffee was required to put her in good form. The new guy was starting today, and she would make *damn* sure her manager knew what a mistake he'd made not choosing her.

Whoever this guy was, he would not show her up.

4

"DAMN ALANA. DOES SHE not own a single pair of pants?" Quinn muttered under her breath as she walked into the Cobalt & Dane head office, tugging on the hem of another one of her friend's dresses.

Thankfully, this little black number covered her more comfortably, although the hem was still above her knees. She'd thrown on a pair of white high-top sneakers and a denim jacket in the hopes of dressing the outfit down. However, judging by the raised eyebrows aimed in her direction, she'd failed.

"You can't sit here." Owen Fletcher, her colleague and friendly office pain in the ass, dropped down into her chair before she had a chance to dump her satchel there. "This desk belongs to a grumpy pink-haired lady who never wears skirts."

Smirking, she sipped her giant latte. "That's got to be the first time you've ever called me a lady."

"Seriously, what's with the dress? It's…weird." He scrunched up his nose as if she'd walked into the office wearing a trash can.

"Can't I wear a dress without getting hassled?" She tugged on the hem again.

The tight fit was already bugging her, not to mention the fact that she'd had to go commando because she hadn't brought a fresh pair of underwear with her. How did women dress this way? Give her a baggy top and a pair of jeans any day.

"Please come to work in a 'Space Invaders' T-shirt tomorrow." Owen got out of her seat and held it out so she could sit down. "You're messing with my view of the world."

"Your view of the world?"

"Yes, the things I need to believe in order to know the universe is right. Taxi drivers are crazy, the Mets are the greatest team on earth and you dress like a teenage boy."

"I guess I should feel honored that I feature in the world law according to Owen Fletcher." She swung her chair around to face her desk. "Now go away. I have work to do."

"No dress tomorrow, promise?" Owen raked a hand through his blond hair and grinned.

"Promise." She shooed him away with one hand and typed her password into her laptop.

Already her inbox was filled to bursting with banal requests. Printer errors, missing cables, password resets and setup for the new hire. *Ugh.*

She couldn't take this job much longer before she'd go nuts. The years she'd spent at university could not be wasted on constantly advising people to restart their computers.

"Quinn?" Her manager, Rhys, came out of his office and over to her desk.

"Morning, boss," she said, pushing up from her

chair. "Any chance you might be free to catch up today? There's something I'd like to discuss."

"Hold that thought. I have a special project for you to work on." He motioned for her to follow him through the IT department. "Bring your laptop."

Great. What'll it be this time, a server upgrade? Someone broke a macro? A busted scanner?

She opened the cable lock that secured her laptop to the desk and tucked the device under her arm. Scooping up her coffee with her free hand, she hurried after him.

"So I was thinking about the position you applied for recently," he said.

"Oh. Really?"

Rhys nodded to the receptionist as they walked past her and into an empty conference room where they usually met clients. "I know you were disappointed you didn't get it."

"No shit," she muttered as she pulled up a chair and placed her laptop and coffee onto the table.

He held up a hand as he usually did when Quinn was about to start ranting. "We had a better candidate."

"Did you really drag me out here to reinforce the idea I'm not good enough?" she asked, heavily ladling on the sarcasm.

He folded his arms over his chest and took the seat across from her. The wall clock ticked loudly in the pause, the sound grating on her nerves. She inspected the remains of her black polish and made a mental note to locate the bottle of remover she kept in the IT department cupboards.

A smile tugged at the corner of his full lips. "Now, if you could dial back the sulky-teenager act for a minute, I'd like to talk about the job I have for you."

"A job?" She tried not to appear too excited at the possibility that they'd already realized she was promotion-worthy without her having to convince them.

"I want you to work a case with the new hire."

If she'd been able to pop Rhys's head with sheer mind power at that moment, she would have. "What?"

"We've assigned him to a case involving a leak at a game design company, and we thought it would also be a great opportunity for you to stretch your wings." He folded his hands in front of him on top of the table.

"What exactly will 'stretching my wings' involve?" She chewed on the inside of her cheek.

"It will mean playing nice in the sandpit, for one." Rhys looked at her pointedly.

"And?" She kept her face neutral, undecided how she felt about this opportunity. It was what she wanted… kind of. However, being forced to work with the guy who'd gotten the job she deserved was not at all her cup of tea.

"Getting a positive outcome. We're briefing the case this morning, so you'll be up to speed on all the important details."

"Can't I work with one of the other guys? What about Jin or Owen?" She drummed her fingertips against her bare thigh. "Surely they'd do a better job with this case since they already know how we do things around here."

"No." Rhys turned his phone over in his hands and swiped at the screen. "This is the opportunity I'm giving you. Take it or leave it."

"Since when do you play hardball?"

"Since you decided to argue with me. I like having you on my team, Quinn, but damn, you're difficult sometimes." He laughed, shaking his head. "Now, are you on board or not?"

She rolled the proposal around in her mind. Her gut told her she'd be stupid to turn it down. Rhys was trying to make things right *and,* given he was the head of IT, she'd still be working for him.

"Who's going to cover my job while I'm on this case?"

He shrugged. "We'll get a temp in."

"Will you let them sit at my desk?" She shuddered at the thought of someone touching her things.

"Yes. Where else would they sit?"

Crossing one leg over the other, she leaned back in her chair. "Do I get a raise?"

"We'll talk about it if the assignment goes well."

"Do I get an office?"

Rhys laughed as if she'd asked for a life-size statue made of marshmallows to be erected in her honor. "No office. What you get is the opportunity to do something different, which I believe is what you've been hounding me for. Do it well and *then* you can negotiate with me."

"Okay."

"Okay?" He stifled a smile as he checked the clock. "You're not going to chase the new guy away?"

"If he's chased away so easily, he probably isn't a good fit for our team," she said. "So, when do I start?"

"Right now." Rhys motioned to the conference room door as Jin, one of the senior security consultants, held the door open for the person behind him.

"Hey, Quinn, glad you could join us."

She opened her mouth to respond but the words evaporated right off her tongue as the new hire walked through the open door.

The intensity of his blue gaze hit her immediately, followed by the sharp cut of his jaw, the tangle of dark hair and broad shoulders. Magic hands...hands that had been on her all night long.

Jin closed the door behind them. "This is Aiden Odell, our newest team member."

AIDEN THANKED HIS lucky stars the FBI had trained him to be calm in a crisis. And finding out Quinn was his new colleague definitely counted as a crisis. Not only because he'd been pissed that she'd sneaked out without so much as a "so long, thanks for the laughs," but also that she'd now see him as a liar and a fraud.

In his defense, he'd tried to come clean but she'd shut him up with her "this is just sex" spiel. Though, judging by the daggers she was shooting at him now, she must have forgotten that little nugget of information.

"Quinn Dellinger is our IT support guru, but given her unique skill set, we've assigned her to this case," Jin said, motioning for Aiden to take a seat at the conference table. "She studied game design at university and has strong ties with the gaming community."

"Nice to meet you," Aiden said, sticking out his hand.

She let it hang there for an excruciatingly awkward moment, only accepting the gesture when Jin cleared his throat. "You, too," she finally said.

"I believe you've already met Rhys?" Jin continued and Aiden nodded. "For your benefit, Quinn, Aiden will be working in the security consultant pool with myself, Owen and the others. But he's mainly going to focus on the information and cybersecurity jobs, so he'll be reporting to Rhys."

Quinn looked as though she'd eaten something sour. But Jin proceeded as if nothing was wrong and ran them through the assignment with Third Planet Studios. There wasn't a whole lot of extra information than the briefing Aiden had been given when he accepted the position at Cobalt & Dane, but the extra run-through was welcome since his brain was still clogged with memories of Quinn's naked body.

She sat across the table from him, scowling, and the sexy little stone in her nose glinted in the light from the window behind her. Her brown-and-pink hair was piled on top of her head, a few strands escaping messily at the sides. What would happen if he withdrew the pin holding her hair in place? He already knew how silky and soft it would feel against his palms, or swishing over his chest as she rode him, her small breasts bouncing with each thrust—

"Aiden?" Jin peered at him from the head of the table. "Did we lose you there for a minute?"

You can't blow it on day one, dumb ass. Pay attention to the job, not the girl.

"Just thinking about the case."

Jin nodded. "It would be great if you could give Quinn a quick intro to your background before we dive into the approach I've put together."

He swallowed, trying to ignore how intently Quinn was staring at him. No doubt she was eager to hear what he did for a living, since it was clear he wasn't a game designer, as he'd told her.

"I've been with the FBI since I graduated. I started out in their police force, primarily working in the New York headquarters." He sucked in a breath, trying not to let the memories get to him. "Then, two years ago, I moved into the Cyber Security Action team. I worked on a number of high-profile cases there, including taking down a prominent financial crime ring."

"Why did you leave the police side of things?" Quinn asked, her tone more than a little accusatory.

"I no longer met the physical requirements for the job." He touched his ear. "I was involved in a shoot-out inside a building, and I suffered acoustic trauma in my left ear. I failed the audiometer test."

She uncrossed her arms and fiddled with the hem of her dress. "Oh."

"I'm partially deaf in one ear and...it's permanent."

He remembered delivering the news to his father. Rather than asking how Aiden was coping with the change, his dad had immediately set about ordering the FBI to provide him a new job somewhere. Anywhere.

The perks of your father being the head of Intelligence. Too bad he'd never put that kind of effort into being a good dad.

"But my injury won't affect my job here," Aiden said. "I do my best work with computers and one-on-one interviews."

Quinn shifted in her seat. Not many people knew about his hearing problem outside his family and the people he'd worked with at the FBI. Certainly no one he'd taken to bed. It wasn't that he was ashamed of it, but he didn't draw attention to it, either. He didn't want sympathy, and he certainly didn't want people thinking he was weak.

So he'd learned to cope, always taking a seat first— as he'd done with Quinn last night—so he could use his good ear. In groups or in noisy venues, he relied on his other senses for context. He read lips, analyzed gestures, listened to pitch and tone if the words themselves were hard to make out. For the most part, he could be around someone every day and he or she wouldn't realize anything was wrong with him.

But even his father hadn't been able to bend the FBI Police's hearing rules. The audiometer test was an unforgiving SOB.

"Thanks, Aiden." Jin nodded and fired up the large screen at the head of the room.

An hour later they were all up to speed with the plan for the Third Planet Studios assignment. Quinn would go undercover as a game designer—since she was the only one on the team who'd actually studied game design and had enough knowledge to pass muster with the employees—and Aiden would go in as himself. He would rattle the cage by interviewing staff and asking questions. Meanwhile, Quinn would keep her ear to the ground to observe the fallout.

They would work together. Closely.

"Is this your first time going undercover?" Aiden asked Quinn as they wrapped up the meeting.

"Yeah." She pushed up from her chair and snapped her laptop closed. "I'm not all that adept at lying. Maybe you could give me a few tips?"

Rhys walked toward the door with Jin. "Excellent idea, Quinn," he said, clearly missing the intended sting in her words. "Take Aiden for a coffee and get to know one another. I'm sure he could give you a few pointers."

A blush flared across her cheeks, lighting up her porcelain skin. Her jaw clenched, the muscle twitching enough that he could tell she was grinding her teeth. "I've got a meeting scheduled with Addison about the new password requirements."

"I'll take care of it." Rhys paused in the doorway for a moment. "Unless you're having second thoughts?"

She steadied herself. "I'm not."

Rhys and Jin left them alone in the room, and the air stilled. Tension rippled across his skin, heightening his senses. Firing up his brain. This was the calm before the storm.

"You...liar," she spat, her eyes flashing. "I can't believe I fell for your bullshit story. Game designer, my ass. Did you know I worked here? Were you following me?"

"Whoa." Aiden held up a hand. "For starters, I tried to give you the truth last night, and you stopped me because it was 'just sex.' Second, I wasn't following you. I'm not a goddamn stalker."

"*I* stopped you," she scoffed. "I thought you were going to lay down ground rules, not tell me you'd been pretending to be someone else. You didn't try that hard to set the record straight."

"When we stopped outside the hotel room, I was going to tell you."

"So you say." She tugged her denim jacket closer around her small frame. "How can I believe anything that comes out of your mouth?"

"You weren't exactly up-front about where you worked, if memory serves me correctly." He walked around the table to cut the distance between them.

"Keeping my private details to myself is *not* the same as lying." Her fists clenched at her sides. "You flat out lied to me. Did you think you'd have a better chance with me if I thought you were a gamer?"

"No." He shook his head, a dull ache spreading out

from his temples as the ringing in his ears from his tinnitus started up. "That's not why I lied."

"Enlighten me, then." Her small pink lips pressed into a flat line.

This was going downhill. Fast.

You can lie to protect a life and you can lie to protect your country, but you cannot lie for personal gain.

His father's words swirled around in his head. He was the only man Aiden had ever met who managed to break the gray areas of life into fragments of black and white, assigning rules here and there so that he always had a framework for making decisions. The habit had stayed with Aiden, and while his moral code might not match everyone else's, he stuck to it.

No matter what.

"I was there doing research for this assignment. I wanted to see if anyone was talking about Third Planet Studios or the leak about their new engine." He rubbed at his temple. "I had a suspicion that Alana Peterson might have been involved since she has such a grudge against them."

Quinn reeled as if he'd slapped her. "So you approached me because Alana's my friend. You acted like you had no idea who she was."

"I was doing my job."

"Your job started today, *not* last night." There was a slight shake in her hands as she fiddled with a button on her jacket. "Did you sleep with me to get information?"

The horror on her face made his stomach churn. He was a lot of things, but he didn't use women in that way. If Quinn had given *any* indication that she knew what was going on with Third Planet Studios, he would have kept talking to her until he got what he needed. But he wouldn't have slept with her to do it.

"That was all real, I promise. I was attracted to you. I wanted to sleep with you. And you seemed pretty into it, as well."

"I can't believe this." Her fingers fluttered at her throat as if searching for something that wasn't there. "You tricked me."

"I didn't trick you into staying the night." He ground the words out. "You were there because you wanted to be."

She swallowed and sucked in a deep breath. "You're right. I did want to be there. But it sure as hell won't happen again. If we're going to work together, you can keep your hands to yourself."

"Fine." He held his hands up, palms facing her. "Does that mean we have a truce?"

"I wouldn't go that far." She narrowed her eyes at him. "I'll work with you on this one assignment because I want something out of it. But I don't trust you, and the second it's over, I'm going to steer clear of you."

"At least you're honest," he muttered.

"It's more than I can say for you." She tucked her laptop under her arm and headed for the door. "Come on, I've been told to take you for coffee."

5

TODAY COULD HAVE been everything she wanted, but instead it was a pile of stinking irony and bad luck. The universe hated her, she was sure of it. But what could she do, cut off her nose to spite her face? She wanted this promotion, and she wasn't going to let some lying phony take it away from her.

Some superhot, crazy-skilled-with-his-mouth phony. *Ugh.*

A little voice in her head reminded her that she had, in fact, stopped Aiden from talking about himself. She told that voice to shut the hell up. Instead, she found a free table in the far corner of the café, but even the familiarity of her favorite coffee spot didn't soothe her nerves. Normally, the Brunswick Café was her safe haven, a place where she could bring her laptop and get away from the drama of the office. The guy behind the bar—who had long hair, tropical-fish tattoos and a broad Australian accent—knew her order by heart.

Even the sight of the quirky meme-inspired posters on the wall didn't make her smile.

Behind the anger she'd hurled at Aiden was a kernel of fear taking root deep in her psyche. Had she been played by yet another guy? Used and exploited and made a fool of? Again.

Now you know he can't be trusted. So work with him but don't let him near you.

"One double-shot vanilla latte with a sprinkle of cinnamon." Aiden put the towering coffee down in front of her. "Sounds like it has as much sugar as it does caffeine."

"Something has to get me out of bed in the morning."

He took the chair opposite her, his own coffee cup dwarfed beside hers. "You didn't seem to have too much trouble today."

She ignored the dig. "What's that? Baby's first coffee?"

"It's a macchiato. A *real* coffee, not some cupcake masquerading as a drink." His full lips quirked up. "I am sorry about lying to you, you know. I really was going to tell you last night."

"Easy for you to say that now." She wrapped her hands around the coffee cup and relished the warmth seeping into her palms.

"You have every right to be angry at me. But I am serious about this job, and I want us to be able to work together." He brushed a stray black curl from his forehead, and Quinn's heart jumped.

Stupid, traitorous body.

Sipping her drink, she focused on the sweet, sugary flavor instead of the way he was looking at her.

"I understand that I'll need to earn your trust back and I'm willing to do that, but not at the cost of this assignment. I'm going to figure out this leak whether you're with me or not." He crossed one ankle over his knee, taking up all the free space at their cramped little table. "I do what has to be done for the sake of the job. If that involves crossing a line or two, then so be it."

The smooth black wool of his pants curved around muscular legs. He wore a plain blue shirt a few shades lighter than his eyes, the sleeves rolled up and the top button popped open. She knew everything that was underneath that shirt— the ridges of muscle, the sharp V at his waist, the dusting of hair across his chest.

How good he tasted.

"I see you take yourself seriously," she said, swallowing another mouthful of her drink.

"I take my *job* seriously."

The ambient noise of the café filled in the gaps of their conversation. Familiar, busy sounds—like the rumble of the coffee machine and the clacking of cups being stacked—soothed her. They gave her something to focus on other than the swirl of toxic doubt in her mind. Quinn tapped her sneaker against the leg of the small table between them, playing out the hyped-up drumbeat of her heart.

This guy seriously unnerved her.

"What tips do you have for me, Mr. FBI? Do I need to know how to defuse a bomb with a paper clip?" She set her coffee on the table again and crossed her legs, keeping her hands at the hem of her dress so it didn't rise too far up her thighs. "I played a lot of 007 back in the day. I'm handy with a gun… Well, a PlayStation one, anyway."

"You need to know how to lie," he said. "Convincingly."

Talk about taking the wind out of her sails. Since she'd given him hell for lying to her, she couldn't exactly proclaim to be a master liar herself. Truth was she didn't often have to lie because she never shared details of her life. But she'd be going undercover as a Third Planet employee in a few days' time, and she'd have to lie to everyone she met.

"Are you going to be able to do that?" He leaned forward, his forearms braced against his thighs until it felt as though he'd closed the world in around them.

Her jaw worked as she ground her teeth together, a terrible habit she'd picked up after "the webcam incident" two years ago. She often found herself doing it when she felt backed into a corner, even though Aiden wasn't the one putting her in this position. This was her opportunity to get the job she wanted, but it drove her full steam ahead to the boundaries of her comfort zone. Hopefully, she wouldn't crash into a wall.

"Quinn, it's part of the job. If you're not going to be able to do it then speak up now and I'll go in by myself."

"No." She folded her arms across her chest and shoved the uncomfortable feelings aside. "I can do it."

The crease in his forehead softened, his lips twisting slightly. "You get used to it."

"The lying?"

He nodded. "Yeah. I find it's easier when you have a clear understanding of why you're doing it. We're trying to stop someone doing bad things, and if we have to lie to achieve that, then so be it."

"I'm glad you can so easily justify it," she muttered. "But some of us were brought up to tell the truth."

"I was brought up to protect those who can't protect themselves. Are the criminals we go up against honest?"

"Comparing yourself to a criminal probably isn't the best way to go."

He sighed. "All I'm saying is that sometimes you have to bend the rules a little to get the right outcome. If you can't handle that, then you're in the wrong job."

Quinn's mother hadn't given her many rules growing up because she could hardly enforce them when she was always at work. But the one thing her mother had stressed was honesty. *Say nothing if you prefer, but don't lie to me*, she'd always said. Her mother had been lied to by Quinn's father, who'd turned out to not only have a whole family he kept tucked away in another state, but a drug problem, as well.

She'd been wary of liars ever since.

"I can handle it." She nodded to herself.

"Good, because it looks like we're partners."

"For now."

QUINN WASN'T GOING to make it easy for him, that much was certain. It was Friday evening and after a full week on the job, he'd barely seen her. There was always an excuse for her to be somewhere else. She rejected or ignored his meeting invites and the only time she ever turned up was if the invite came from Rhys or Jin.

He leafed through some papers on his desk, sorting out his research and notes on Third Planet Studios. Quinn would have to face facts soon. As of Monday morning she would be going undercover. He would also be doing some digging around after-hours, keeping his presence minimal for a day or two until Quinn had been able to integrate herself into the team. Which might be tough since she was prickly as a porcupine.

Kind of funny how that turns you on, isn't it?

"Hey." Logan walked by his desk, interrupting his thoughts. "Good to see you."

He motioned for Aiden to follow him into the Cobalt & Dane boardroom. It felt a little strange knowing his friend was the head of this entire company. He still remembered all the pranks they pulled as kids. In fact, his father had taken to calling them the Terrible Twosome while they were in elementary school after they managed to upend an entire classroom's worth of furniture.

Still, Logan was extremely passionate about his company and the work they did. Aiden would *not* let his friend down.

"I've got a few minutes before my next meeting so I thought I'd stop by and see how your first week went." Logan shut the door behind them.

"It went well. I'm glad to be here."

"How's the ear?"

Out of habit, Aiden touched the bad side of his head. The ringing had become a part of his life, and some days it bothered him more than others. But he made a point never to complain, not even if it made him want to put a fist through a wall. "It won't affect my job."

"That's not why I'm asking." Logan narrowed his eyes at Aiden as he set up his computer at the far end of the conference table.

"In that case, I'm fine."

"Okay, okay." Logan held up his hands. "You're a difficult bastard, aren't you?"

Aiden grinned. "You knew that before you hired me."

Logan looked up from where he was plugging his laptop into the AV cable for the boardroom projector. "All ready for Monday, then?"

He nodded. "Ready as I'll ever be. Wherever that leak is, I'll find it."

"That's what I like to hear."

They chatted for a few moments until Logan's assistant interrupted them to usher in a new client. On the way out, Aiden bumped into Rhys.

"How's the assignment going so far?" Rhys asked, toying with a security cable in one hand as they walked.

"Great. I've arranged to go in and chat with the owner about seven on Monday evening. He said the staff keep pretty odd hours, so the office is never really empty." He shrugged. "But he'll shoo everyone out. That'll give me a chance to go over the employee files."

"How do you think Quinn will do?" Rhys studied him closely, his dark eyes giving nothing away. Aiden felt as if he was being tested but on what, he couldn't be sure.

"Why don't you ask her yourself?"

"You'll keep an eye out for her, won't you?" Rhys fiddled with the combination lock on the security cable. "She'd never ask for help and she's exceptionally capable. But this is a different environment for her and you're a little more seasoned."

"Of course." He nodded. "But for the record, I think she'll be fine."

"Me, too. But we take care of our own here, Aiden. I won't be so corny as to call us a family, but this isn't just any company you're working for."

"Understood. I'll look out for Quinn without letting her know it."

"Good man." Rhys added, "I expect a quick resolution to this. It's an important assignment but we're fully tapped at the moment, and Logan has big plans for you."

What was Rhys trying to say? Was it common knowledge that he and Logan Dane were old friends? He sure as hell didn't want people thinking that he'd only gotten this job because of his personal connections. Truth was, Logan had been pestering him to come across for a year, not the other way around.

But experience had told him that people with tall-poppy syndrome didn't care about the facts. They'd tear him down here like his colleagues had done at the FBI because of his father.

"Of course," Aiden said, swallowing his doubts and putting on his best poker face.

Rhys nodded and made his way to his office, leaving Aiden to mull over his choice of words. Logan had assured him that no one would take their friendship as a sign of nepotism, especially since most of the employees in the company had come through referrals. As head of Cobalt & Dane, Logan had tight control over the hiring process. With the work they did, it was of the utmost importance that he trust every single employee.

And Logan trusted *him*. Simple as that. But a doubt niggled somewhere in a deep, dark corner of Aiden's mind. Would he have to try to shake the privilege tag and battle the opinion that he hadn't gotten here on his own merit all over again?

Outside, the sun had dipped and the city lights were beginning their nightly spectacle. Inky-blue bled into the fading orange of sunset. He'd lived in New York all his life but the skyline never ceased to amaze him. And while he preferred the relaxed vibe of his Brooklyn brownstone neighborhood, Manhattan's lights were something else. Like a pirate's treasure scattered across the sky, diamonds carried by the wind.

"Not a bad view, is it?" Pink flashed in his periphery.

"It's all right, if you like that kind of thing," he quipped.

Quinn stood close enough to talk to him but far enough away not to invite any physical contact. Her tiny frame was swamped with an oversize black T-shirt bearing a dizzying pattern of pink skulls and crossbones. A gash split the fabric of her tight black jeans midthigh. Her hair hung in a long plait over one shoulder, the pink-and-brown strands neatly woven together.

"I do." She bounced on the balls of her feet. "It's kind of beautifully unattainable."

Poetic. That was unexpected. Quinn was a complete enigma, one that he couldn't shake the desire to figure out.

"Is there anything I can help you with?" He tried for a businesslike tone but judging by the way she sucked on her lower lip, it had come across as cold. "Are you all set for Monday?"

"Yeah." She bobbed her head, wrapping the end of her plait around her finger. "I… Uh, are you going to be there?"

"Not until the evening. I want to give you a chance to settle in."

"Sure. I wanted to know when you'd be in so I can keep my distance."

He raised a brow. "How come?"

"Well, we don't want people to suspect that we're…" She paused.

"On the same team?"

"Yeah."

For the first time since he'd started at Cobalt & Dane, she reminded him of the Quinn he'd first met. Adorably awkward, a little unsure of herself. Vulnerable.

He wanted to scoop her up and tell her everything would be okay. But that was not only inappropriate given their current situation—and her anger toward him—but he knew that it would only push her further away. She needed space to trust him again…if she ever decided he was worth it.

"Act like you normally would if it was your first day at a new job. Introduce yourself to people, stick to your script and don't take any notice of me. If you actively try to avoid me, that could seem suspicious, so pretend I'm not there." He stifled a smile. "You've been doing a pretty good job of that all week."

Her lip twitched. "Would you buy it if I said I was practicing?"

"Not a chance."

"See, honesty suits you." Her eyes tracked his face.

"Why are you talking to me now?"

"I wanted to make sure we were on the same page… you know, for the assignment." She traced patterns with the toe of her purple high-top sneakers. "And Rhys said I had to check in with you."

"Are you nervous?"

Her eyes avoided his. "Maybe."

He packed up his desk, tucking his laptop into his satchel and stacking two disposable coffee cups in one hand. Quinn followed him into the kitchen, where he dumped his trash.

"There's nothing to worry about. Rhys wouldn't be putting you in there if he didn't believe that you could do it." He leaned against the kitchen table. "It's no different than starting a new job. Be your charming self and make friends."

"You say that like it's the easiest thing in the world."

"It is. You love games. They love games. Pretend

you're at a convention and you're talking to people while lining up for something."

She laughed and hitched her backpack higher up on her shoulder. The straps were decorated with pins that appeared to be from various gaming events. "I never talk to people in lines."

"You talked to me at the cocktail party."

"And look how that turned out." She shook her head, a blush staining her pale cheeks.

"Pretty good, I'll say." Aiden crossed his ankles and braced his hands on the edge of the table. "Despite what happened the next morning, I don't regret that evening at all. I had a great night with you."

She made a *hmm* noise that could have been agreement or skepticism; he wasn't sure. There appeared to be a fine line between those two things when it came to Quinn.

"Do you regret sleeping with me?" he asked.

"I think I should have stuck with Leafina." The words were chosen carefully, perhaps so she could avoid lying without actually revealing anything to him. "Trees make good friends, you know. They don't spill your secrets and they don't argue with you."

"Why would an honest gal like you have any secrets?"

The change in her expression was akin to the aftermath of a flash of lightning; one moment filled with light had suddenly plunged into darkness. Her brows crinkled and her bottom lip caught between her teeth. She ran her tongue over where she'd bitten herself, smearing a drop of blood.

"So I'll see you on Monday," she said, hooking her

thumbs under the straps of her backpack. "If I'm still around in the evening."

Without waiting for a response, she turned and left the kitchen, disappearing into the office and leaving Aiden wondering what the hell had happened.

Just because she doesn't lie doesn't mean she's not hiding anything.

6

QUINN ACTIVELY AVOIDED the nightmare of starting a new job. She'd only ever had three jobs—selling burgers at a fast-food chain through high school, her first tech job in a computer store, where she sat in the back and fixed PCs, and then Cobalt & Dane.

She hated leaving the comfort of a known environment. What if the boss hated you? What if you sucked? What if your colleagues decided to single you out?

Kind of like how you singled Aiden out on his first day?

A sliver of guilt made its way into her gut but she rationalized it away. Aiden was the one who'd fooled her, so the situation with him was different. He wasn't some innocent guy rocking up to a job totally unaware.

If anything was true about Aiden, it was that he was totally aware. Of everything.

Like how he'd zeroed in on her nerves last night. Or the way he'd seemed to sense she was hiding things from the world. She'd never met someone who seemed to be able to figure people out so quickly. How did he do it?

"You don't have to stay all night because it's your

first day." One of her new colleagues—Jason...or was it James?—said as he walked past her desk. "We try not to work the newbies into the ground right away." He flashed her a wide smile and looked her up and down.

"It's fine. I have one thing to finish off before I go." Her eyes darted to the door near the now-empty reception desk. Still no Aiden. Where was he?

They'd left the plan open as to whether or not she'd see him tonight, but the truth was she didn't want to be left out of the action. This was her chance to shine, so she couldn't leave now.

The office was clearing out. Hopefully, by the time he arrived there wouldn't be anyone left to catch them together.

"Don't stay too late."

Quinn smiled tightly. "I won't."

"See you tomorrow, then." He hovered for a moment before leaving.

Only a few people dotted the funky white-and-green desks. The office had been decked out in the company's colors, with small earthlike orbs hanging from random sections of the ceiling. Quinn counted four life-size statues of game characters in her immediate vicinity. A clear glass case near the reception desk held awards and memorabilia.

So far the people at Third Planet Studios seemed nice enough. They'd given her a desk, encouraged her to put a few personal belongings down and had shown her around the facilities. Did any of them suspect she was lying about her identity? Thankfully, a fake surname and LinkedIn profile were all she needed for her cover, and she'd kept her first name to ensure she responded to anyone who called out to her.

They'd kept her job history pretty similar, too—the less false information she had to remember, the better. Lying, it turned out, was a complicated business.

"You're still here." A deep voice broke her out of her thoughts.

"You're not supposed to be talking to me," she said under her breath, her eyes flicking around the room to check if anyone was within earshot. "Not with people around."

"Relax." He seemed totally at ease with their situation. "Walt is kicking everyone out now."

Quinn, on the other hand, could have snapped the edge of her seat for how tightly she was holding it. She balled her hands into fists and then released them the way her therapist had taught her.

"This is cute." He leaned over and reached for the fluffy llama she had on her desk—the lone personal item she'd brought with her.

"I won it at a convention."

He inspected the small stuffed toy. "What's his name?"

"Palmer."

"Palmer the llama? Really?"

She stifled a laugh. "I never said it was a good name."

Aiden placed it back on her desk and walked away, shaking his head. For the first time all day, her heart didn't seem to be thundering in her chest, her hands weren't shaking and her breath appeared to be coming and going at a normal rate.

Her eyes followed him down between the neat rows of desks. Dark denim hugged his strong legs and perfect ass. He wore a white shirt, but it was tucked in, highlighting his trim waist and the broad expanse of his back. Dark, curly hair brushed the top of his collar, wild and messy enough that her fingers ached to touch and tug.

Heat flittered low in her belly as she remembered what he felt like on top of her, inside her. Covering her. Pleasuring her.

"Stop it," she muttered under her breath as she watched him disappear into the boss's office.

But the images wouldn't go away; it was as if he'd tattooed them on her brain. Eternal torture of the sexiest kind. Why couldn't he have been any other guy... particularly one that she didn't have to work with?

She couldn't hide the truth from herself. She was oh, so ready to repeat their night in the hotel. Every single kiss, every lick, every touch—she wanted it all again.

Stupid libido. She hadn't heard from it in two years and then all of a sudden it became a deafening roar in her ears. Didn't it know she had a job to focus on right now? Talk about an inopportune time to make a comeback. Her sexual hibernation period appeared to be over, thanks entirely to Aiden.

Go home to your vibrator and take care of it yourself. Much safer.

"Quinn!" her "new boss" called from the depths of his office. "Can I see you for a minute?"

She jumped up, flustered and filled with raging heat. "Yes...uhh, just a minute."

Swigging her water bottle, she fanned herself furiously with one hand and hoped to hell her face wouldn't be the same color as the streaks in her hair. The last thing she needed was to appear anything but one hundred percent professional.

Putting one foot in front of the other seemed tougher

than usual, as if she'd used up all her brain cells today and now her body was compensating by obliterating her motor skills.

"I've gone around the office and sent everyone home, so there's no need to worry about anyone seeing you here now," he said as she entered his office. Aiden was already inside.

Walt Dixon seemed an unlikely name for a guy who headed up a hugely successful video game company, but one look at the man and it was clear he was in the right job. A white T-shirt featuring a concept drawing of one of the characters from their latest game, "Occupant Z II," stretched across his protruding stomach. His office walls were heavily lined with signed game art, stills and industry photos. Figurines were arranged in one corner of his desk, a little cluster of blood-spattered zombies and heavily armored fighters. An enormous stuffed pink unicorn toy sat in the corner of the room, staring at her with unblinking eyes.

"I'm going to leave you both to your own devices this evening because it's my little girl's birthday. But I've given Aiden all the access he needs to look around." Walt toyed with the end of his frizzy ginger-and-gray beard. "I know it was only your first day in here, Quinn. Still, did anything come up?"

She shook her head. "Not yet, but I'm definitely keeping an eye out."

Walt nodded and handed her a card. "You've both got my number if you need to ask me anything tonight. But I'd appreciate if you saved it for only the most important stuff."

"We won't interrupt your family time unless it's absolutely necessary," Aiden said with a nod. "I'll be coming into the office tomorrow anyway, so I'm sure any questions can hold over until then."

"I appreciate it." Walt grabbed the jacket from the back of his chair. "Now, if you'll excuse me, I have a toy to deliver." He picked the unicorn up by its rainbow-colored mane and strode out of the room.

"It's not every day you see a big, burly guy like that carrying a unicorn." Aiden tilted his head.

"You clearly haven't been to many cons." Quinn shoved her hands into the pockets of her black skinny jeans. "I've seen a guy bigger than him dress up as a My Little Pony."

"No way."

"Yep." She nodded. "He rocked it, too. I've never seen a sassier version of Rainbow Dash anywhere."

"I've missed out on the whole con experience. I should go to one." He narrowed his eyes in mock seriousness. "But there's no way in hell I'm dressing up as a pony."

"I figured you more for a Powerpuff Girl." She smirked. "Blossom, I think. Pink is definitely your color."

He stepped closer and put his hand on the desk next to her. "I would rock the shit out of the Powerpuff Girls."

"That may be the sexiest thing anyone has ever said to me." Laughter bubbled up in her throat, dissolving the tension and stress of her day.

"I'm not threatened by the color pink," he said, reaching out slowly, gently, and touching the end of her braid, his thumb stroking over the dyed strands mixed in with her natural brown ones.

"I can see that." Her breath stuttered.

She waited for the nerves to kick in, the anxiety and wariness that normally accompanied having someone this close to her. But nothing came. Aiden dropped her braid.

"I'm going to get this search started," he said, pushing up from the desk. "I don't want to be here all night."

"What do you need me to do?"

"Nothing. You're free to go." He held the door open for her as they exited Walt's office. "You did your duty today."

"Oh. But Walt said he'd cleared everyone out so we could look around." She flicked her braid over her shoulder, determined not to be left out of the action... At least, that was what she told herself.

"Yes, but I'm running point on this assignment. And I'm saying you can go home." He thrust his fingers through his dark curls, and Quinn's blood thrummed.

"You're *running point*?"

"Yes." He dug a hand into his pocket and pulled out his phone, checking it briefly before putting it back into place. "I'm the senior consultant and you've been assigned to assist me."

"Isn't Rhys in charge?" She shot him a look as she checked the desk closest to her, gingerly leafing through a few papers left on the desk. "I don't answer to you. I answer to him."

"While we're in the field, you answer to *me*." His blue eyes narrowed, their color suddenly seeming less like a warm summer sky and more like an iceberg. "It's important that you respect that."

"Spare me the male-pride act," she scoffed.

"The fact that I'm male has nothing to do with it."

"Enlighten me, then, oh great one. Why *are* you in charge?"

"I'm in charge because I'm more experienced."

The words made her cheeks burn. "So Rhys told me when I found out you got the job and I didn't."

"I didn't know you applied for this job."

She shrugged and didn't say anything further.

"In any case, I've done this before, and I know what happens when things go wrong." A shadow crossed over his face, a hint of the past. A secret. "You need to follow my direction so we're on the same page and so I can make sure nothing bad happens to either one of us."

"Because I can't look after myself?"

"No, but this isn't just about you. I don't expect you to trust me yet, but I do expect you to follow my lead while we're working on this assignment." He started toward the HR office. "If you're not comfortable with that then have a chat with Jin. Maybe they'll let you work with another consultant."

"That will only make me seem difficult. I don't have much of a choice, do I?"

QUINN FOLLOWED AIDEN into the office of the company's HR manager. But he left the door open in case someone returned to the office unannounced.

He'd been anxious to see Quinn all day, to the point that he'd been distracted in meetings and fumbled his words when Jin had thrown him into a brainstorming session. Not like him at all.

Women didn't rattle his cage the way Quinn had. Usually, he was the cool, calm and collected type. Unattached. Good for a fun time only. He wasn't against relationships per se, but they didn't fit into his life. His job had always come first and what little time he had to himself was divided among his friends, family and a few hobbies.

The women he'd dated had all been quickly pissed off at their low priority in his life. But he hadn't promised them anything more. He figured he had years ahead of him to worry about finding a partner; for now he was on a mission to get his career on track. To make a name for himself that didn't come with the privilege of association.

But Quinn had blown his neat, consistent list of priorities right out of the water after only one night.

"Are you sure you don't want to head home? You've been here all day," he said, ignoring the part of him that hoped she'd stay.

"I'm not going anywhere." She bounced on the balls of her feet. "What are we looking for?"

She'd toned the Quinn-ness down for her first day undercover, swapping ripped skinny jeans and sneakers for neater black jeans and a pair of low-heeled ankle boots. On top she wore a fitted black tank top and a leather motorcycle jacket. The combination gave her a sexy, kick-butt ninja vibe.

"I asked the HR Manager to set aside the employee files of anyone who's faced disciplinary actions in the last twelve months." He gestured to the neat stacks of files sitting on top of the filing cabinet. "We're going to go through them and look for anything that might suggest the person has a grudge against the company. If he or she does, put that file into a separate stack, and that will form the basis of my interview list."

Bobbing her head, she made her way to the pile marked A–D. "I'll start here."

"Actually, do you mind if I take the A's?" He tried not to cringe. Normally, he was on his game enough that he positioned himself with his working ear facing out. "That way you'll be on my good side."

For a moment she looked as though she was going to offer some sympathetic comment, but instead she said, "So you're Mariah Carey all of a sudden?"

He laughed, relieved. "Yes, you may only take photos from my best angle."

Shaking her head, she switched places with him. "Is everything we need in these paper files?"

"I don't think so. Only things that have been printed out as part of the recruitment process and anything that requires a signature, like a disciplinary action." Aiden took the pile next to her. "But it should be enough to help me when I start interviewing the staff tomorrow."

"What makes you think they'll talk to you?" She scanned a document. "I wouldn't."

"They might not say much, but their bodies do the more valuable talking anyway."

"Did they train you to read body language at the FBI?" Her voice held a note of wariness rather than the curiosity that most people had when asking about his career.

"Yeah. It's important for a lot of reasons, especially when you're interviewing people." He pulled another file from his stack, his finger catching the edge and flipping it open.

"Do they teach you how to lie?"

He took a moment to formulate his response. "They teach us to read body language and how we might be accidentally giving information away."

The building's air-conditioning hummed in the quiet

room, and the rustle of papers beneath his fingertips highlighted her lack of response. He scanned the page— it contained notes from a disciplinary action for a minor security breach, password sharing. Aiden set the file aside in the pile for employees of interest.

"I can teach you a few things, if you'd like," he said, turning toward her.

She pulled another file and kept her eyes straight ahead. "About body language?"

"Yes, how to read it." His eyes drifted over her as she worked, her slim fingers flipping through the documents. The chipped black nail polish was gone, replaced with a pink color bright enough to stop traffic.

"Maybe some other time." She narrowed her eyes at something in the file and she handed it to him wordlessly, and he placed it on the growing interest pile.

"Correct me if I'm mistaken, but you seem kind of preoccupied with people lying to you."

She stiffened. "Preoccupied?"

"It sounded more palatable than *obsessed.*"

"I am *not* obsessed." She finally looked up at him, her eyes simmering. "Is it so wrong that I want people to be up-front with me?"

"It's not wrong, but it does tell me that there's a reason for your behavior." Satisfaction took root in his stomach when her expression confirmed his statement. "That's why you blew up at me for lying about my job even though I tried to explain it to you. And, if we're being honest, it was kind of inconsequential to what we did anyway."

She gaped at him. "Inconsequential? Your lies meant I ended up sleeping with someone I work with."

"Hold on a minute—" He held up his hand. "You

weren't exactly Little Miss Honesty with me, either. If you'd mentioned that you worked at Cobalt & Dane, I would have pulled the pin."

"Oh, so I'm supposed to trust you because of that?"

"No, you're supposed to take responsibility for your part in what happened. You slept with me because you *wanted* to. I didn't trick you into it." He forced a slow breath.

He closed the file in front of him. Why the hell should he care what she thought of him? It was obvious her feelings were rooted in some deep hurt that had nothing to do with their night together. She was damaged by something. Afraid.

Her tongue ran across her lower lip, leaving it shiny and pink.

"What do you want from me?" he asked.

Burning hunger flared across her face. A delicate flush rose up her neck, and her lips parted. Tempting as sin. Heat blazed in her hazel eyes, lighting up the flecks of gold and green in her irises. Frustration and anticipation, excitement and a hint of fear. All competing for dominance.

It was how she'd looked at him that night, as she'd taken his hand and followed him to his room. As she'd watched him lower himself down onto her body, then latch his mouth onto the sweet spot between her legs. Tasting her. Drowning in her.

"Quinn." He tried to hold his response back and hide it from her. "Don't look at me like that. If you do…"

"What?" she asked, the question echoing in his head, bouncing around.

"Do you want me to be honest?"

She blinked, eyes wide and black as an abyss. "Yes."

The air snapped around them, filled with chaotic energy and magnetic desire. He took the folder from her hands, tossing it onto the HR manager's desk.

"I'm sorry I lied," he said.

She backed up against the filing cabinet, her chest rising and falling beneath the open motorcycle jacket. "And?"

"I wish you hadn't snuck out that morning." His training and practice slipped away, the skills he'd honed to be detached and impassive dissolving like a snowflake on his tongue. "I wasn't finished with you."

A whimper escaped her lips. "I had to go."

"I know." He slid a hand along her jaw until his fingers threaded into her hair. "But I've thought about you every day since then. I've imagined what else I want to do to you, what else I want you to do to me."

Her teeth scraped along her lower lip as her palms came up to his chest, her fingers sliding along the fabric of his shirt and setting off sparks within him.

"Tell me to stop." His forehead came down to rest on hers, his eyes squeezed shut. "Because I'm going to kiss you if you don't."

7

USE YOUR WORDS, Quinn. Say it, say something. *Anything.*

But she couldn't. Trapped between the hard metal cabinet and Aiden's even harder body, his hand wrapped around the base of her skull, she couldn't convince herself to put a stop to it.

His warm breath fanned out across her cheek as he hovered, his lips so close to hers. Damn it. She wanted this kiss, wanted it like sleep at the end of a long day. She wanted to sink into him and let the world fade away until there was nothing but his tongue against hers. She wanted *not* to be terrified of feeling like this.

What happened to baby steps? It was supposed to be one night, spontaneous and risk-free and—

"Just say the word." His lips brushed her cheek.

Her breath stuck in her throat and her heart pounded like a fist against her rib cage. Awareness ran through her, filling her with a delicious tingling.

"Quinn," he breathed as his lips crushed down on hers.

The force of his kiss pressed her hard into the cabinet, the files rattling inside it as the handle dug into her back. But the glide of his tongue between her lips, the pressure of his hands and the warm, heady scent of him took everything else away. Robbing her of all experience but his kiss.

Her body responded immediately, an aching pulse gathering hot and tight in her sex. Fingers curling into his shirt, she clung to him with all the desperate, terrifying need she'd locked away for the past two years. But Aiden wasn't going to take advantage of her like her ex; he wasn't going to use sex to humiliate her.

Strong hands held her head in place as he explored her, taking and giving all at once. Memories of him swirled so vividly in her mind it was hard to tell what was real and what wasn't. His pushed his thigh between her legs, parting her and pressing against the pulsing ache there. She gasped.

Yes, yes, *yes*.

"Damn," he moaned into her ear as she ground herself against him, shameless in her desire.

The seam of her jeans rubbed her through the thin cotton of her panties, giving her enough friction to drive her crazy but not enough to give her what she needed. Heat flared within her as his hand breached the hem of her jacket, pushing the leather out of the way so he could skate his hand up her rib cage to cup one breast in his palm.

A groan broke the air, but she had no idea who it came from. His thumb teased her nipple through the fabric of her tank while he kissed her neck, zeroing in on the spot where her pulse fluttered wildly.

Teeth. Tongue. Lips. He used them all.

Hooking a finger over the edge of her tank, he pulled the fabric down along with the soft lace cup of her bra until her breast was freed. The second he touched her sensitive nipple, her back arched, her head lolling against the metal filing cabinet.

"My God," she moaned.

Each not-so-gentle flick of his thumb across her nipple sent heat spiraling through her, but his hands weren't enough. She fisted his hair and dragged his head down to her breast, flooded with relief when he took the swollen bud between his lips. Pleasure and pain bled together as he nipped her with his teeth, soothing the spot immediately with his tongue.

She didn't realize his hand was at her waistband until cool air hit her skin when he dragged down the zipper of her jeans. Slipping his hand inside, he pressed the heel of his palm to her sex, rubbing in slow, circular movements as he mimicked the motion of his tongue. He laved her nipple, alternately sucking and licking until she felt as if she was going to explode.

"You're far too good at that," she gasped. "Tell me that wasn't part of your James Bond training."

"Search and seduce?" His throaty chuckle vibrated against her chest as he moved from one breast to the other. "Breaching enemy lines?"

He slipped his finger beneath her panties, grazing her sex. Blood rushed in her ears as his fingertip pressed against her entrance, teasing her. Testing her.

His mouth found its way back to hers, wet and hot and open. "Nothing could have prepared me for how good you feel. So silky and perfect."

Her muscles clenched as he slid a finger inside her, easing it in and out while he continued to massage her with the heel of his hand.

"You're so tight," he whispered into her ear.

Reaching out to him, she brushed her fingertips along the hard ridge of his erection.

"Damn, Quinn." He pressed against her hand and thrust his finger into her again. "You drive me crazy."

Stars danced behind her eyes, and each stroke dragged her further under. The ragged edge of his voice obliterated her, the catch in his words revealing how turned-on he was.

"You're so close." His lips peppered her jaw with kisses. "I can feel you shaking. I want you to come against my hand."

The words were more than she could take, the husky sound and the expert touch tipping her over into oblivion. Her thighs quaked as she came, her knees giving out so that he had to hold her up with his free hand until her climax subsided.

What the hell did you do, Quinn?

Reality crashed into her like a stone-cold tidal wave. Her eyes snapped open, searching the roof of the HR manager's office.

Not again. Please, please, please *don't let there be a camera.*

She wriggled out of Aiden's grip, extracting herself with flustered force and wrenching his hands from her. Her breath came hard and fast as she checked each corner of the room. There didn't seem to be anything that might have recorded their tryst…unless they had put secret ones in the smoke detectors. Would they do that?

"Quinn?" Aiden reached out for her but she stepped back, clipping her elbow on the corner of the filing cabinet and yelping in pain. "Tell me what's going on."

"I… We…" She rubbed her elbow and let out a deep

breath to dislodge the panic blocking the words from coming out. "We shouldn't have done that."

He watched her without managing to give a single thing away. Damn him and his stupid body-language training. "Why?"

"Oh, I don't know, maybe because we're on a job together at our client's office? Or perhaps because there could have been…there could…" She fought the rising tide of emotion clawing its way up her neck.

"Try to breathe slowly." He pulled the chair out from behind the manager's desk and held it out toward her. "Sit."

The last thing she wanted was for Aiden to see how weak she was. How anxious. Talk about giving him ammunition to prove she wasn't up to the task. One orgasm and she was about to have a full-blown panic attack.

"Sit." His voice left no room for argument, which made her want to do the opposite of what he ordered.

But the floor shifted beneath her feet, and her face tingled. If she didn't sit she might faint…and then she'd never be able to show her face at work again.

"I'm sitting because I want to, not because you're telling me to," she grumbled as she slid her butt into the chair and leaned forward, bracing her head between her knees like the therapist had taught her.

"I don't give a shit so long as I don't have to carry your unconscious body out of here." He spun the chair around and squatted down in front of her so they were at eye level. "I have to admit that's the first time a woman's ever had that reaction after I've given her an orgasm."

She cringed. Maybe it was time to get the word *damaged* tattooed across her forehead in big black letters.

At least that way guys would steer clear of her from the get-go. Then she could save herself the mortification.

"You don't have to give me the whole story." He put a hand on her shoulder, his touch steady and comforting. "But can you at least tell me if you're okay?"

"It's not you," she muttered into her hands. "I should have been able to control myself."

Maybe if she stayed in the brace position long enough, he would leave. But she could see the buttery-smooth leather of his shoes and the soft denim of his jeans. He hadn't moved an inch.

"Control is overrated." He removed his hand from her shoulder. "Would a glass of water help?"

She nodded, without revealing her face. Not because she wanted a drink, but because she needed a moment alone. To deal with the shame and embarrassment, to work herself up to looking him in the eye.

This was why she couldn't do anything more than a one-night stand—it seemed she could only keep her shit together for a single encounter. Where there was no risk of getting hurt. After that the fear started to creep in. What if it happened again? What if she trusted him and he used it against her?

She swiveled the chair back and forth on its wheels, as if she could shake the crazy out of herself. When would she go back to being a normal girl who could enjoy more than a one-night stand? Probably never.

She slowly sat up, letting her balance settle before she pushed out of the chair.

"Here." Aiden reappeared with a glass of water, holding it out to her like the proverbial olive branch. "Drink it slow."

"Yes, sir." She managed a weak smile and sipped the cool liquid, her heart slowing to its normal pace.

"It's probably time to get you home." He straightened the files they'd taken from the cabinet and scribbled a note on a sticky pad.

"But we didn't get past *G*." Quinn pressed the cool glass to her temple and sighed.

"Doesn't matter. I'll come early tomorrow and finish it." He paused, rubbing the back of his neck. "And your health is more important than sorting through files."

"My health is none of your concern."

"While I'm in charge of this assignment, *any* consultants who are working for me are my concern." He motioned for her to follow him out of the room. "Whether I make them orgasm or not."

"Are you trying to give me a heart attack?" She drank the rest of her water, and they passed through the kitchen so she could put the glass into the dishwasher. No evidence, just in case. "We're not allowed to talk about us sleeping together or that…kiss."

"We're allowed, but you don't want to."

This day was not going according to plan. Proving herself and keeping things professional with Aiden had been a big fat fail. Where was the reset button when she needed one? At the very least she could use a checkpoint in order to replay the past few hours… Hell, why not redo the last week and a bit while she was at it?

They took the elevator down to the building's lobby in silence. She was grateful that he wasn't pushing her to explain why she'd flipped out; it wasn't a story she'd shared with many people. Alana and her therapist were pretty much it. Even her own mother didn't know.

Quinn couldn't bear the thought of her mother hearing that despite her best efforts, she'd raised a naive fool.

Outside, the traffic rushed past. The peak hours were over but New York was still jammed full of people. Rain fell, lightly misting the street until it developed a glossy sheen and amplified the sound of tires turning and people hurrying past.

Aiden stuck a hand out to signal a cab. "Come on, let's get you home."

"You don't have to accompany me." She folded her arms across her chest and resisted following him as the cab pulled up to the curb. "I can get home on my own."

"You almost passed out up there," he said, opening the passenger door. "I wouldn't be a good colleague if I didn't make sure you got home safe."

Colleague. Thinking of him that way soothed her edges a little; it was nonthreatening, equal. And didn't imply any of the unwanted attraction that she felt toward him.

The rain caught in his hair, dampening the dark curls until they shone like polished onyx. Her sex clenched, the muscles remembering what it felt like to have the heel of his palm pressed against her. Massaging. Pleasuring.

Now that there was space between them and air to breathe, her body relaxed…and with relaxation came the slow trickle of desire.

Could you be any more screwed up? It's not normal to flip from mind-blowing orgasm to panic attack and back again just like that. He probably thinks you're a freak.

"Quinn, we're both going to be soaked. Let me do the right thing."

If they split the cab it wouldn't bust her budget for the week, and she really couldn't deal with the subway right now.

Sliding into the backseat, she gave the cabbie her address…well, the house a few doors down from her address. Aiden might not be like her ex, but that didn't mean she could trust him.

AIDEN WALKED THROUGH his front door and let out a long breath. His clothes had dried out on the ride to Quinn's place—or at least the address she'd given the cabbie. He'd asked the driver to wait so he could make sure she got inside her house okay, but she'd stood in the rain, arms folded over her chest, until he'd given up. For all he knew that wasn't even her street.

But she wasn't the kind of girl who could be pushed. Someone had hurt her really bad, and now she wore her scars like armor against the world. The girl had baggage with a capital *B* and that was so *not* his thing. He hated drama.

Then why was he inconceivably drawn to her? Maybe it was that whole moth to a flame thing? He wanted the bright, shiny light even though he knew he'd get burned.

Stupid. He should never have kissed her, never mind that he couldn't think about anything except how amazing she'd felt in his arms that first night.

"You're not the brightest crayon in the box, are you?" he muttered as he walked into the living room and slung his satchel onto the couch.

"It's all right, A. Not everyone can be the brightest crayon." His brother's voice made him jump. "But you're still my favorite."

"What the hell are you doing here?" He really didn't have time for Marcus's problems tonight. Not when he needed at least eighteen cold showers to calm his libido down.

"Can't a guy stop by to check in on his little brother?" Marcus grinned and tugged on the end of his sleeve, a gold cuff link winking in the light.

Dress sense aside, Aiden and Marcus looked so similar, many people thought they were twins despite the three-year age gap between them.

"You only stop by when you want something."

"I got what I wanted." He held up a glass with at least three fingers of Scotch in it. Neat.

Not a good sign.

"What's going on?" He sagged into the couch, and Marcus poured him a drink.

"Tess had to come by the house to collect a few things," he said stoically, as though he wasn't talking about the wife, who was currently in the process of leaving him…and breaking his heart. "I needed to make myself scarce."

Marcus might not have had Aiden's FBI training, but they'd both learned a lot from their father about keeping their feelings hidden from the world. If emotional suppression was a sport, Graham Odell would take gold, silver and bronze.

"And you came all the way here? I thought you didn't leave the island unless it was in a first-class seat."

Marcus handed the glass over, a crack finally appearing in his perfect facade. "I couldn't deal with Dad and his lectures about 'moving on' tonight. I want to drown my sorrows in peace, if that's okay with you."

"My Glenfiddich is at your service." Aiden tipped

the glass up to his lips and relished the soothing taste as the amber liquid slid down his throat.

After the night he'd had, a drink was definitely in order.

"Distract me," Marcus said, taking the single seat on the other side of the coffee table. He crossed one ankle over his knee, his black woolen suit pants extending up his leg to reveal a pair of patterned socks. "How's the new job going?"

Well, I slept with my colleague the night before I started and then tonight I got her off in our client's office. Then she had a panic attack. It's great, just great.

"So far, so good," he replied.

"That bad, huh?" His brother smiled and crossed his arms. "What did you do?"

"I'm reserving the right to pass judgment until I've been through a whole assignment. It's only been a week and a bit." He shrugged and went for the Scotch again. "Time will tell."

"What's telling is the fact that you're guzzling that drink like it's your last."

"And how many have you had so far? Two? Three?"

"The woman I devoted my entire adult life to is leaving me. I'm entitled to get drunk." Marcus pressed his lips into a flat line. "Is it Dad who's put you in a shitty mood?"

"Nope, because to do that I would have needed to speak to him."

"Ahh, still avoiding him, I see." Marcus shook his head. "But you're the Last Hope."

Their father liked to command and control everything in his life. Aiden, Marcus and their sister, Candace, had been expected to fall in line with his plans over the years. But the ultimate pressure always landed on Aiden when his older siblings disobeyed.

Hence the nickname, Last Hope.

"What's the point of talking to him? He's still pissed I decided to move on after he got me that gig in the Cyber Security team." He snorted. "Apparently, by taking charge of my own career I'm throwing it back in his face."

"God forbid you don't bow down at his feet for the privilege of following his life plan." Marcus shook his head and loosened his tie. "At least you won't have him breathing down your neck at the new office."

"It'll be nice to do good work and not have people assume I'm getting ahead because of my name." At least, he hoped so. He traced the rim of the glass and thought back to Rhys's comments about Logan having big plans for him. He hadn't *seemed* disingenuous when he'd said it.

But it was early days yet, and he wasn't going to reveal his relationship with Logan if he could help it.

"Now you should get yourself a personal life."

"Says you."

Marcus laughed. "Seems the workaholic gene is strong in our family. I called Candi on my way over and she was still in the office. I told her not to stay too long or she might come home to find her husband packing his bags and crying neglect."

The lines around his brother's eyes deepened and his jaw clenched, and for a moment Aiden thought Marcus might actually crack. But a second later the creases smoothed out and he sipped his drink as if nothing was wrong.

"It's not your fault, Marcus. She never seemed to

mind that you worked crazy hours when you were taking her to Tiffany's."

"Too right." His brother sighed and raked a hand through his dark hair. "All I can say is, find yourself a nice simple girl who won't give you any trouble. The complicated ones can't be fixed, and they take up too much head space."

Marcus was only talking out his current pain; Aiden knew Marcus would do anything to have his wife back. But Aiden couldn't help but think of Quinn with her trust issues and closely held secrets. His brother had a point; Aiden didn't have time for anything serious with her. If he had any hope of proving to his father why he'd gone out on his own, work had to come first.

"They say they love you," his brother continued, waving his Scotch glass around so that the liquid sloshed against the edges. "But you have to remember that what they say is one thing and what they mean is something else. They don't even know they're lying."

Aiden turned the words over in his head. As much as he wanted to focus on his brother, the case tugged at the edges of his mind and he thought of Alana Peterson. Quinn had seemed certain, that night at the party, that her friend was only going after Third Planet for their lack of female representation. But what if that was a cover? What if Quinn was perpetuating a lie and she didn't even realize it?

"You can't listen to them, man." Marcus downed the rest of his Scotch and set the glass down, motioning for him to top up their drinks. "They'll lead you down the path to disaster."

8

THE THIRD PLANET STUDIOS office looked totally different in the middle of the day. The place had a buzzing energy that bordered on contagious. Aiden found himself smiling as he watched two people argue passionately while sketching on a whiteboard. Zombie game design was a serious topic.

He'd been interviewing people for the past four days, dutifully working through the employees of interest. But so far, no one had anything interesting to say. And Quinn had done her best to avoid him, which wasn't surprising. But he wasn't about to let that continue. They needed to talk about what had happened the other night.

Having finished up his meeting with the Human Resources manager—a cheerful woman named Joan Hoxton—he was due to start interviewing the last group of employees. But he wanted to clear the air with Quinn first.

"You were in early this morning," Joan commented. "Normally, I'm the first to arrive."

"We're committed to getting a good outcome on this assignment, Ms. Hoxton."

"Please, Joan is fine." She smiled. "I've scheduled meetings with the remaining employees from your list. Walt had to make a statement to the employees about the leak and why you're here, but he's calling it a minor security breach at this stage. We haven't been specific about what information has been leaked, so if you could refrain from sharing that, we'd appreciate it."

"Not surprising," Aiden said as they walked from her office out to the meeting rooms. "We suspected my presence would spark questions." That meant it was time to start shaking the tree with a little more vigor.

"You don't need to interview me, do you?" Joan asked with a teasing tone.

"Have you stolen any information from the company?" He raised a brow.

"No, sir. I'm afraid video games aren't really my forte."

"Well, then, we should be fine."

As he walked with Joan, he spied Quinn sitting at her desk. With pink earbuds plugging her ears, she bobbed her head to the beat.

He wondered what kind of music she listened to. Pop? Rock? Obscure German death metal?

She looked up and caught his eye, her deer-in-headlights expression socking him in the chest. Why was she so fearful of him? Who had hurt her so badly to make her act that way?

Before he could think how to react, her eyes were back down on her computer screen. But the bobbing had stopped, and she sat as still as a picture apart from her fingers flying across her keyboard. She had a wall around her stronger than steel, and stupidly he wanted to break it down with his bare hands.

"How long have I got before the first meeting?" he asked.

"About forty minutes."

"I'm going to get a coffee from the Starbucks around the corner. Would you please ask Quinn to meet me there in a few minutes so I can talk with her?"

"Of course." Joan gave him a conspiratorial wink before bustling off like a woman on a mission.

He would have preferred not to have anyone in the know other than Walt and Quinn, but the Third Planet Studios owner was determined to keep his HR manager in the loop. From what Aiden could tell, Joan seemed the least likely person to leak information on a game design engine. Still, his experience had taught him that criminals didn't have a type; they came in different shapes, sizes and colors, and the less he assumed, the better off he would be.

By the time he'd made it to Starbucks, lined up, bought two coffees—one real, one cupcake drink—and found a spot in the back of the store, Quinn walked in.

"You wanted to see me?" she asked, her eyes darting around the café to make sure none of her "colleagues" were there.

"Make yourself comfy." He gestured for her to sit and he handed her drink over. "Disgustingly sweet, just the way you like it."

Her eyes darted up to the ceiling, checking each corner methodically as if she'd done it a thousand times before.

"Are you scared of cameras?" he asked, a theory developing in his head. One he hoped to hell wasn't true.

She squirmed, sipping her coffee as she fingered the lengths of her brown-and-pink hair. Today she'd worn it down except for a little section pinned by her ear with a tiny pink skull and crossbones. For the first time since they'd met, she had makeup on, a thick smudge of black under her eyes that almost concealed the puffiness there. But he didn't miss that tiny detail.

"What do you want?" she asked, ignoring his question.

"First, I wanted to see if you were okay after…the other night. You've been avoiding me."

"I'm fine."

"I'm sorry if I pushed you. I didn't mean—"

"You didn't."

"What?"

"Push me."

God help him, it was like pulling teeth. "I don't think I've ever said this to a woman before, but can we talk about it?"

"No need to talk. I'm fine. You're fine. Everything's *fine.*"

Everything was so *not* fine, but Aiden had learned long ago that sometimes you had to know when to let go of a line of questioning. He sighed. "How is everything with the other employees? Have you heard anyone talking about the leaks or the engine?"

She shook her head. "No, they've been talking about you, though."

"Tell me."

"The other girl who works on game design thinks you're hot." A smile tugged at the corner of her lips. "She said she'd be your Princess Peach any day of the week."

"Jealous?" he teased.

"Yeah, right. Only in your wildest dreams, Mr. FBI." She swigged her coffee.

"What about the other staff?"

"Not sure you're their type. Don't take it personally."

They didn't really have time for banter but he'd take Quinn teasing him over the look she'd given him earlier. "Any comments on Walt's announcement?"

"Minh said he thinks the breach is a cover for something else, and Zach…" Her cheek hollowed as she chewed on it.

"What about Zach?"

"He said we should all refuse to speak to you. Zach is scaring people into thinking they're going to get fired." Her fingers skated around the edge of her T-shirt, rubbing back and forth against the ribbed neckline. "I'd be careful with him."

"Zach," he muttered as he checked the list of meetings he had scheduled for the day.

Sure enough he was on it. Zachary J. Levitt. Game designer and user-experience champion…whatever the hell that meant. Two disciplinary actions: one for use of abusive language online when identified as a company representative, and an incident with a design intern. Complaint withdrawn.

Interesting. "What do you know about this guy?"

"Not much." She shrugged, her nose wrinkling. "Uhh…"

Damn, she was cute when she did that. *Eye on the prize, Odell. You're here to do a job, remember?*

"Where does he sit in the office?" He started with a benign question, a tactic he often used with skittish interviewees.

"Next to me."

"Okay, so you must be able to give me some details about him. What have you two talked about?"

"Other than video games?" Her tongue darted out to catch a stray droplet of coffee off the rim of her cup, and his body hummed. That mouth had been on his mind all damn week.

Snap. Out. Of. It.

"Not a lot. He keeps asking these fishy questions, trying to find out where I live." Her dark brows crinkled. "He told me I was the first woman they'd hired in a while. Apparently, some intern who used to work here had a meltdown and mysteriously they haven't had many female employees since."

Some intern? Perhaps the same woman who'd made a complaint against him.

"Name?"

She shook her head. "He didn't say."

Aiden braced his palms against his thighs. "Anything else?"

Quinn opened her mouth but then she snapped it shut. Too bad he didn't miss a thing.

"Out with it," he said.

"You remember my friend Alana from the party?"

"How could I forget?"

A soft noise came from the back of her throat. "Well, you know I mentioned she's been chasing Third Planet for a while because they never have any strong female characters in their games? Wouldn't surprise me if Walt was a not-so-closet sexist."

"I'm more interested in why Zach felt the need to bring up the intern with you." He hadn't even met the guy and already he had a bad feeling about him.

He was familiar with the guy's type. Flaunted his

privilege over others, self-incriminating but too damn cocky to worry about it. Grade-A jerk.

"He said that I should stick with him because he's a good guy and that he could help me get ahead at Third Planet." From the look on Quinn's face, she was as disgusted by it as he was. "He said the intern didn't last because she didn't understand how things worked around there."

"Which is how?" His nails dug into the thick denim of his jeans, about ready to tear holes in the fabric if he wasn't careful.

"Apparently, I have to understand that it's about 'give-and-take,'" she said, making quotation marks with her fingers. "And he's earned the right to take."

"He's not taking a *damn* thing from you." He ground the words out through gritted teeth, fighting to quiet the seething roar inside his head. "Make your way back to the office and I'll follow in a few minutes. I'll be speaking to him today."

"Aiden." Quinn held up her hands, her cheeks pale and her eyes glittery and wide. "You can't repeat what I said. I still have to work here until we figure this out. I don't want to reveal us *or* antagonize him."

"I'll do more than fucking antagonize him." He balled his hand up into a fist so tight the joints of his knuckles protested. "If he so much as lays a hand on you, I swear to God I'll tear him apart."

Whoa. Since when did Aiden go from zero to caveman in under a minute? He sucked in a breath and held it until his lungs felt as if they might burst; then it came out in a satisfying *whoosh*.

"If he lays a hand on me, he won't have a hand for very long. Now, if you're ready to blow our cover, then go ahead and repeat what I said." She pushed up from the table and crossed her arms, daring him to argue. "Or you can keep your big mouth shut."

"Since when are you the levelheaded one?"

"I'll take that as a win. Score one, Pink." She touched her fingertip to her tongue and drew an imaginary line in the air.

"You're still at least negative seven," he called out after her, but the saunter in her gait told him she wasn't giving him an inch.

About five minutes later, a text came through on his phone from Quinn.

I can look after myself, but thanks for the gesture.

There wasn't a shred of doubt in his mind that she could handle herself, but it killed him that she'd been put in a position where she'd have to.

However, he couldn't let it occupy him. He had an assignment to complete and a rat to sniff out. Ruminating over Quinn's past—and trying to figure out why he had this sudden compulsive desire to protect her—would have to wait.

"WHAT DID THE cabbage say?" Zach asked as Quinn came back to her desk after taking a call from Rhys in one of the meeting rooms.

It was lunchtime and most of the staff had gathered in the kitchen or gone out to get a bite. But not Zach. It almost seemed as if he'd waited for her.

He leaned back in his chair, cold gray eyes running up and down her body, as they often had over the past two days. Scooting his chair closer, he rested an elbow on her desk. Invading her space.

There was no way in hell she'd give him the satisfaction of letting him see how uncomfortable he made her. "The cabbage?"

"Yeah, big beefy guy with no brains." He jerked his head toward the meeting room where Aiden now sat. Alone. "A cabbage."

The insult prickled under her skin. "How would I know? I didn't talk to him."

"I noticed you took a call in the room next to him. I figured you did it so you could listen in and see who's getting fired."

"I don't think he's firing anyone."

Zach stretched his bony arms above his head. "Probably leaves the dirty work to someone else. He must be too important for that."

"Jealous?" The word slipped out before she could stop it. So much for not antagonizing him.

"Hardly. I graduated at the top of my class, Harley Quinn."

Her skin crawled at the nickname he'd given her without asking if she wanted it. "I bet your parents are proud."

"Of course they are. What parents wouldn't want a child like me?"

From her vantage point, Quinn watched as Aiden poked his head out of the meeting room. It wasn't fair how her heart skipped a beat when his eyes swept over her. The assessing gaze was not dissimilar to the way Zach looked at her, minus any of the calculating intimidation or sleaziness, of course.

One action, two intents. That made all the difference,

but for a long time she'd been unable to distinguish between the two. She'd grouped everyone in her life into two categories: her ever-shrinking personal circle and everyone else.

"See, it's obvious by the way he hangs on to the door frame he's trying to show off." Zach made a disgusted noise in the back of his throat. "Don't tell me you're one of those pathetic girls who goes crazy for a guy with muscles."

If only he knew. "I don't go for anything."

"Does that mean you're off the market?" His eyes snapped toward her. "You sure don't act it with all… that."

That was a pair of fitted jeans with a rip at the knee. She gritted her teeth. "My relationship status has nothing to do with my work here."

"Single, then."

She wanted to rip the smug look off his face with her bare hands. "None. Of. Your. Business."

"*Very* single." He rolled back to his desk on the opposite side of their pod, chuckling to himself. "Duly noted."

How had this guy *not* been fired for sexual harassment? Her knuckles ached before she even realized she'd clenched her hands into fists. If she had anything to do with it, Zachary J. Levitt would be eating dirt… preferably from a dusty patch of ground far, *far* away from her.

Aiden reached their desks by the time Quinn calmed down, though she stuck her headphones in and pretended she hadn't noticed him. Not that his presence could ever be so easily ignored. People dodged out of his way as he walked, giving him space and room to move. Though whether it was because he was a guy—a *big* guy—or because he exuded confidence and authority, she wasn't sure.

She tapped the button on her phone to pause her music, but she left her earbuds in so Zach and Aiden wouldn't realize that she could hear them.

"I don't have to go anywhere with you," Zach said. "I have work to do."

"It's just a chat, one that your boss has given me authority to execute." Aiden rested his hands on the edge of the low wall behind their desks. At first glance he might appear to be stopping by for a friendly chat, but the way he tilted himself forward spoke volumes about his desire to show Zach who was boss. "There's nothing to be afraid of."

Quinn gave a little cheer in her head but forced her eyes to stay on her computer screen. Zach shoved his chair back so hard it knocked into hers.

"How about you keep your temper tantrum to a minimum and show your colleagues a little respect?"

The words on her screen blurred into one another; she couldn't concentrate while Aiden and Zach were having a pissing contest next to her. She plucked one of the buds from her ears.

"Is there a problem?" She shoved Zach's desk chair back toward him.

"Don't you worry your pretty little head," Zach replied. "This'll be quick."

He stalked out of the pod and headed toward the meeting room. Aiden's eyes flashed like blue lightning when she caught his gaze. He sucked in a breath—his chest expanding and collapsing in a way that made her fingers itch to touch him. Soothe him.

"Let it go," she said softly as she popped her earbud in and turned back to her desk.

The second that Aiden left, Quinn sagged against her seat. As much as it pained her to admit it, he was damn good at his job. He'd handled Zach with authority and had kept a lid on his temper in the process. She had no doubt he'd be able to tear that little piece of shit limb from limb—in the most professional way, of course— behind the closed door of that meeting room.

"What the hell was that all about?" Another junior programmer, and the only other girl on their team, appeared at her desk like a meerkat popping up from behind a rock.

Quinn pulled her earbud out of her ear again. Seemed she wasn't going to listen to much music today. "Just two guys trying to beat their chests."

"I'll put my money on the new guy." Natalie grinned, her red curls bouncing as she plonked herself on Quinn's desk. "Seriously, though, you've got to watch out for Zach. He's a loose cannon."

"What do you mean?" She tried to act casual.

Natalie's eyes darted around. "He's got a reputation for being a little rough on female programmers."

"So why is he still here?"

"He's Walt's nephew." She shrugged. "After the last time, Walt gave him a talking-to…but I think it only made him better at covering his tracks."

"The last time?"

"You didn't know?" Natalie blinked at her. "The last intern we had here ended up leaving rather suddenly…apparently, Zach cornered her after work one night when they were alone. Tried to use his relationship with Walt to convince her that she'd have to 'keep him happy' to get ahead in the company."

"That son of a—"

"But there was no proof. No cameras in the offices or in any of the meeting rooms. All that she had was footage of her running out of the reception area like a ghoul was after her." Natalie's freckled legs swung back and forth beneath the hem of a floral dress. "She made a complaint but ended up leaving soon after. I'm not sure exactly what happened to make her drop the complaint."

"Has he done anything to you?"

She swallowed. "He tried a few things but I've got older brothers, so I know how to protect myself. I can throw a punch or a knee. But it didn't come to that, thankfully. He backed off me when Sarah started."

"And he hasn't done anything since she left?"

Her red curls bounced around as she shook her head. "I was worried he might…but no."

"Why not?"

For a moment Quinn thought she might not answer, but Natalie's mouth set into a grim line and she nodded to herself. "You arrived."

9

QUINN HAD TO fight every natural response in her body and talk to Zach when he came out of the meeting room. Hopefully, he would be cocky and stupid enough to divulge some valuable information to her in the heat of the moment…he seemed the kind of person who would do that.

Unfortunately, other than slinging around some unique—and rather creative—insults about Aiden, he had nothing useful to say. So she'd posted herself in the staff kitchen, claiming the need for a change of scenery. But really she wanted to keep her ear out for any tidbits from the other employees as Aiden conducted his interviews.

When the office had mostly cleared out and it appeared as though she'd be going home empty-handed, one of the more senior programmers walked into the kitchen. His name escaped her—something monosyllabic like Tom or John. Or maybe it was Tim.

He had his phone tucked between his ear and his chin as he poured a cup of coffee from the pot, turning toward her.

She forced herself not to look up, instead bobbing her head to an imaginary beat and typing gibberish on her keyboard so he'd assume she couldn't hear him.

"I don't know." His voice was hushed. "They've got some guy in asking questions. He looks like he could be a cop, but he's not in uniform."

As he turned back to the coffeepot, Quinn lost track of what he was saying, her ears only catching chunks of the conversation. She took in his Hawaiian shirt patterned with green leaves, making a mental note to identify him to Aiden.

"I can't…it's classified… I understand. Yes. Yes, I'll get it to you soon."

It wasn't anything concrete, but he seemed nervous as a sheep surrounded by a pack of wolves. He grabbed his coffee and ended the call, shoving the phone into his back pocket as he walked out of the kitchen, leaving her alone again.

Don't draw attention to yourself. Nice and easy, just act normal.

Resisting the urge to call Aiden immediately, she packed up her laptop and notebook. Hopefully, Zach the Horrible—if he could give her a nickname, she'd return the favor—wouldn't be at his desk. There was only so many times in a day she could stop herself from punching a person in the nose.

Back at her desk, her phone rang. When Aiden's name flashed up she caught herself smiling. Which was stupid.

Oh, so stupid.

"Hello?" She answered the phone as if she had no idea who was calling.

"Quinn, it's me. I wanted to check in on you."

"No need." She clicked her laptop into the docking station on her desk, and fiddled with the cable lock while keeping her phone wedged between her ear and shoulder. "I can handle myself."

"I know you can." Pause. "Is there any chance you'd be able to get together tonight? Maybe we can grab a bite to eat."

She bit down on her lip. It would be a legitimate business dinner because she *did* have information for him. While she was contemplating a response, Zach came back to his desk, leering at her openly.

"Sure," she said slightly louder than necessary. "I'd love to. When do you want to meet?"

Better to make it obvious that she had a date than to have to fend off more innuendo from Zach the Horrible.

"How about we catch up in an hour? That'll give us time to get away from the office."

She swallowed against the little bubble of nerves that had started its ascent up her throat. "Why don't we meet around here?"

Aiden might be proving himself to be a better guy than most other men she knew, but she wasn't ready to let him see what her life was like outside work. Manhattan was safe, far removed from her tiny apartment and all the issues she kept locked up there.

"Less risk of getting caught if we go somewhere else. Since we both live in Brooklyn, why don't we find a place there? Then you'll be close to home."

Damn, he had a point.

"Ah, okay, why don't you pick a place and text me the address? I'll meet you there."

"Do you like Italian food?"

"Does Mario like mushrooms?"

The booming sound of his laughter pulled at the corner of her lips, but she forced them back down. This was a business meeting, pure and simple. Nothing wrong with being excited about progress with their assignment. It certainly had nothing to do with seeing Aiden again. She hung up the phone and sucked on her lower lip, forbidding herself from smiling.

Jeez, Quinn, you've got to get a lid on this. The swoony teenage girl act is not a good look on you.

"Got a hot date?" Zach asked as she slung her backpack over one shoulder.

"Just meeting a friend," she replied with a tight smile.

"Where?" His gaze held hers as if challenging her. Would he be the type of guy to show up uninvited? Probably.

"Not sure. He's going to text me the address."

"So it *is* a date."

Maybe she should have called him Zach the Nosy Jerk. "It is possible for men and women to be friends, you know."

"Without sex?" He laughed, the sound firing warnings all through her body. "Not in my experience."

"Well, it is in mine. Good night."

She walked as quickly as she could, hoping that he couldn't smell her anxiety. His type was all too familiar. Entitled. Selfish. Nasty.

Please don't let him follow me out, please don't let him follow me out.

How many times had she told Aiden that she didn't need his help? Right now she would have eaten those words to have someone else with her as she waited for the elevator. Saying Zach gave her the creeps would be putting it mildly.

The elevator dinged and Quinn rushed inside, jabbing at the close button until she was safely locked away. Alone.

AIDEN HAD PICKED Gustoso not only because they made the best carbonara in the state, but also because he knew the owner, and part of him wanted to impress Quinn. If she liked Italian food, Benedito and Carmela's menu would knock her socks off.

He'd taken quite a few dates to the restaurant over the years because he could relax there. Be himself. But this wasn't a date at all. He shook his head as he logged into his Cobalt & Dane email.

This was *work*.

And he had to remember that. This job was an opportunity for a new beginning, for him to build the reputation he wanted. He needed to remain focused.

"How can you concentrate on my delicious cooking if you're working while you eat?" Carmela walked past his table and set down a bottle of water and a glass.

The older Italian lady wore the same floral apron she always did. The thing had to be at least thirty years old. Covered in stains from pasta sauce and flour. But she still managed to smell like fresh-cut parsley and lemons, no matter what she'd been cooking.

"I'll need another glass tonight." He winked at her.

"You have a date?" Her eyes twinkled as she shook her head, the tightly wound salt-and-pepper curls shaking around her face. "*Tesoro mio*, I thought you were going to marry me one day?"

"Benedito would have my hide."

Laughing, she placed a hand on his shoulder. "*Certo*. I'll get you another glass."

"And some bread?"

"*Va bene*. A growing man has to eat."

He didn't point out that he'd reached his full height of six foot one by college. In Carmela's eyes, he'd always be the cocky boy who'd come in to get a gelato every Sunday afternoon. She'd teased him about how the girls giggled whenever he walked in, how they fluffed their hair and preened for him like colorful little birds.

Gustoso had been his safe haven over the years. He'd come to Benedito after his accident to talk through his options with the FBI. Not because the old man knew anything about his career, but he'd cared. More than he could say for his father, who was more concerned with protecting his legacy than with what Aiden wanted. Or needed.

Something brushed his shoulder out of nowhere and he jumped, shocked out of his thoughts. He held his hand up out of reflex and then snatched it back to his lap when Quinn squeaked.

"You frightened me," she said, a little breathless. Her cheeks glowed like pink flowers, her chest heaving beneath her top.

"Sorry, I didn't hear you walk up." He hid his embarrassment by finishing off the email he'd started. "I thought you'd come from the other side."

Her features softened. "Sorry, I forgot you wouldn't be able to hear me. It's a tight squeeze in here." She shrugged out of her backpack and stowed it under the table. "I probably should have taken that off."

Carmela chose that moment to swan past and not so subtly check Quinn out, her lips pursed as she placed a water glass in front of her. "Can I get you anything else to drink? A wine or *aperitivo*?"

"Water is fine." She nodded, her face impassive.

"I'll have a beer," Aiden said.

Carmela nodded, retreating and traversing the busy restaurant as nimbly as a cat. Quinn sighed. "I don't think she's used to pink-haired people in here."

"Lucky you don't have any tattoos."

"I could have tattoos." Her pale fingers dug into the sweet curve of her shoulder as she massaged the muscle there.

"Unless you've gotten it in the last week and a bit, I doubt it. I've seen every inch of you, in case you don't remember."

Just like that his concentration vanished in a puff of smoke. It served him right for trying to bait her. There was no point sending Rhys an email now; he'd have to do it after they finished up tonight because thinking about Quinn's naked body was counterproductive to other things he needed to do...such as stringing a coherent sentence together.

You're letting her mess with your focus. This is your chance. You don't want to make Logan regret the day he brought you in.

"So..." She sucked on the inside of her cheek. "How did the interviews go today?"

"Good." He rubbed a hand over his face, hoping it might wipe clean the memories of Quinn crying out his name. Getting a grip wasn't usually such a problem. "Nothing concrete yet, but I've got a few things to follow up on."

They paused the conversation as Carmela arrived with their drinks and a couple of menus. Quinn was starving, so they ordered right away.

Waiting until Carmela had left the table, Aiden asked

Quinn, "How was Zach after he got back from the interview?"

"He didn't give me anything. Well, nothing useful anyway. He had his rant and then I decided to work in the kitchen to see if anyone else was talking about you."

"And?"

"Lots of speculation but no confessions."

The scent of basil and garlic wafted through the air, and his stomach rumbled. "I doubt they're going to come out with it that easily."

"Maybe." She sipped her water. "But there's something going on. I overheard the guy in the Hawaiian shirt on the phone. He thought I had my headphones in but I could hear him. His conversation sounded suspicious."

"Hawaiian shirt?" He lifted the beer glass to his lips and relished the taste on his tongue as he tried to remember the guy's name. "Yeah, Chris something. I interviewed him today. What did he say?"

"He thought you might be a cop, and he said you were asking questions. He seemed nervous and then he said something about information being confidential." Her adorable nose scrunched up as she paused. "He said he was going to get the person something, but he didn't say what."

"Interesting."

"How was he in the interview?"

"Nervous, but most of them were. Sometimes that comes across as anger or resistance. Sometimes people just have sweaty palms and shiny foreheads."

Quinn leaned forward, open curiosity on her pixie face. "Which one was he?"

"Definitely sweaty palms." Aiden laughed. "I thought

he'd put a hole in his jeans by how many times he rubbed his palms on them."

"Gross."

The conversation flowed easily between them as they traded tidbits of their day. But it was obvious that they didn't have anything solid to take to Rhys, and it had been almost a week since Quinn had started at Third Planet. He knew some assignments took a while to break and they hadn't been at it long, but he'd been told to wrap this one up quickly, and he wasn't about to disappoint his new boss.

Getting some runs on the ground would make it clear that he was there because he deserved to be, not because of his relationship with Logan. A memory bubbled up to the surface, a wisecrack his old boss at the FBI had made once about him being the boy with the silver spoon. The "prize pooch" they'd called him as though he were nothing but an animal trained to do and say whatever his father said.

Aiden shoved the memory aside as the food arrived at their table. Without hesitating, he drove his fork into the pile of *linguini carbonara* and twisted, the wrapped strands creating a tight bundle of delicious cheesy, eggy goodness.

"This is amazing," Quinn said through a mouthful of her *amatriciana*. "I guess I can forgive the old lady's death stare."

"One, it wasn't a death stare. And two, why are you so concerned about what other people think?"

"I'm not." She stabbed her fork into the mound of pasta, sending a little spray of sauce over the edge of the bowl.

"I thought you didn't lie."

She chewed, her cheeks puffed out with the generous forkful. A dot of red sauce decorated the side of her lip, and he had to stop himself from leaning forward to catch it with his tongue. Even eating like a ravenous teenage boy, she was sexy as hell.

"I *don't* care what people think. Doesn't mean I don't wish things were different." She chased a slippery piece of bacon with her fork. "Sometimes I wonder if I'd be better off if I blended in."

"Don't blend in." Awareness thrummed through his body, lighting him up like a carnival at night. Saturating him in the color and vibrancy of her. "I couldn't imagine you without your pink hair and all that attitude."

"I get tired of people assuming I'm not serious."

The vulnerability of her words struck him square in the chest. She may pride herself in being truthful, but she was rarely totally honest and open with people... at least from what he'd seen. And here she was, cracking open the wall around her. Letting him peek inside at the real Quinn.

He wanted more.

"Why do you think people assume you're not serious?"

She drummed her fingers on the table. "I guess they see this woman with pink hair and baggy T-shirts and assume I'm a dumb chick who doesn't know anything. That I'm going through a phase by being the way I am. It's not a phase...it's just me."

"Prickly as hell and damn proud of it."

A smile spread across her lips. "I'm not always prickly."

The hint of sensuality in her words tugged at the core of him, letting his attraction to her burst through like water crashing over a dam. Unleashed and furious. Untamable.

Damn, she was hot. He didn't want to be attracted to her—she had baggage for days, and getting involved with a colleague was definitely not a good idea so early on in his new job. But Lord help him, he wanted her. Every quirky, sexy bit.

He shifted in his seat. "Yes, you do have the ability to turn down the prickle factor."

"I never used to be like this, you know." She attacked another mouthful of pasta, as if keeping her mouth busy would stop the confessions from coming out.

"Why did you change?"

The haunted look that crossed over her face—like a ghost sucking the life out of her—twisted something in his chest. He wanted to know who had caused that look so he could track down the son of a bitch and take him out. He wanted to slay her demons.

What is wrong with you? Have you forgotten the bit where you determined that the job needed to come first? Keep it in your pants and get back to work.

"Let's just say that there's a reason I don't trust people. The last time I did, something really bad happened."

And she had him. Hook. Line. Sinker. "What happened?"

"I might tell you one day, Aiden. You seem less messed up than everyone else, but that doesn't mean I trust you yet." Her eyes were guarded, wary. But he understood her need to protect herself; he respected it.

"We're a team, you know that, right?"

She nodded. "Yes, and *you're* in charge. So we might be a team, but we're not equal."

"Does that bother you?"

"Kinda." A thoughtful expression swept over her face. "I'm used to being an underdog. My mom was an underdog, too. We didn't have a lot when I was growing up. She worked two jobs and I didn't see her much. But I studied hard and ended up at Cobalt & Dane. In her eyes I'd made it big by getting a degree and a real job."

"But you don't agree with that?"

"I've been fixing people's printers and resetting passwords for four years." She cast him a rueful smile. "Not that there's anything wrong with doing that, but I've done my time. I'm smarter than that."

"Isn't that why Rhys put you on this assignment? To give you a chance to step up?"

"I wanted *your* job. I applied for it, but I wasn't good enough."

This wasn't news to him; she'd told him about it already. But now it dawned on him that he'd flown in without so much as a formal interview because the boss wanted him. Just like he'd gotten into the FBI because of his father and then advanced because of the Odell legacy.

In his mind, this *was* a different situation. Logan had come to him, not the other way around. He wasn't accepting a handout. But would Quinn see it that way? Part of him wanted to lock that information up tight. The other part of him knew how she would react if she found out from anyone besides him.

Time to man up and spit out the truth.

"There's something I have to tell you," he said, setting down his fork.

"Okay." She watched him warily.

"Logan Dane is a close personal friend of mine. He's been asking me to join Cobalt & Dane for a while, over twelve months." He paused to let that information sink in. Judging by the way her eyes widened, she hadn't known or suspected his connection to Logan. "I don't believe that information is common knowledge but I wanted to tell you because you mentioned applying for this position. I didn't want you to think that you didn't get the job simply because you weren't good enough, as you said."

Silence. She toyed with her cutlery, her eyes lowered to her plate.

"And, since you've made it clear that honesty is important to you, I wanted to do the right thing."

"Thank you," she said, her voice almost lost in the restaurant din. "So people at the office don't know you're friends with Logan?"

"I don't think so." He rubbed at the back of his neck. "It's not a secret exactly, but I want a chance to put a few runs on the board before it gets out. Some people may assume I only got the job because of my friendship with Logan and not because of my experience or skills."

"They probably would assume that." She nodded.

"It's not true. Logan wanted to hire me because of what I can do and because he trusts me." His stomach churned as Quinn's eyes moved slowly over him. Assessing. Judging. Would she be like everybody else? "And I couldn't stay at the FBI anymore."

"Why not?"

He had to force himself not to grind his teeth. "My father was the head of Intelligence. He always had a say in what work I was doing, what team I was assigned to…it was stifling. I couldn't get any respect for my own work because everyone believed any success I had was because of him."

Her eyes softened. "That would suck."

"Yeah, so I understand the frustration of trying to prove yourself. I get why you would be pissed that I got this position when you wanted it."

A smile curved her pink lips. "Yeah, I am still kind of pissed."

"But you won't hold it against me?"

"I can't. Not your fault you're a 'better fit' for the job than me," she said, making quotation marks with her fingers. "But we'll kick butt on this assignment and then I'll get my promotion."

"I hope you do," he said, and he meant it.

10

THE MINUTES HAD ticked by slowly as Quinn finished her meal, shoving the last forkful of pasta between her lips. What was it about Aiden Odell that made her want to spill her guts?

Perhaps it was because he'd opened up to her, too. As much as she hated that he'd been handed *her* job on a silver platter—while she had to fight to prove herself—he was being honest with her. What if he really had been about to tell her the truth the night they met?

"What are you thinking?" His deep voice broke her concentration.

"Just getting up in my own head."

"You do that a lot, don't you?"

A smile pulled at her lips. "And you don't?"

"Touché." His eyes crinkled at their corners. "But you can tell me what's going on. I can't be the only one getting all deep and meaningful tonight."

God, he looked so damn sexy. So at ease in his environment, like he belonged. She had to fight the urge to reach across the table and run her fingertips along his stubble-roughened jaw.

She was sick of being scared, sick of wanting sex and then feeling guilty for it. Sick of denying herself because some creep had screwed her over.

But how could she admit that she'd been dumb enough not to notice her boyfriend—the one who'd supposedly loved her—was streaming video of them having sex to a bunch of people? Not to mention what had happened in the aftermath…

She squeezed her eyes shut.

"Quinn?" Aiden placed his hand over hers and she forced herself not to flinch.

"I want to be normal," she whispered.

As she wrenched her gaze away from the floor and up to him, she'd expected to see pity. Sympathy. Panic, even.

But what she got was something else entirely. Anger blazed in his eyes like a house fire, terrifying and out of control. All consuming.

The silence absorbed her. For a moment she wondered if he could see what had happened flickering across her face like an old reel of film. Revealing her deepest, darkest secrets.

"Someone hurt you," he said. Not a question, a simple statement.

"Yes." She reached over the table and grabbed his beer, bringing it to her lips and downing it in one long swig. Desperate to drown out the voices telling her she was headed straight for danger. "That's where I learned that I can't trust people."

She was through with people like Zach the Horrible intimidating her, through with missing out on something she'd loved so much before the webcam incident.

Sleeping with Aiden that first night had been a step forward, a test to see if she could change.

A test she'd passed.

"Will you take me home?" She held her breath, watching the uncertainty mixing with lust in his expression. He had hungry eyes, but a wary mouth. "Then you can come up to my apartment."

"I don't know if that's a good idea, Quinn."

"We can play 'Mario Kart.'" She pushed back from the table and reached for her bag. "Or are you afraid I'll win?"

He laughed. "Never."

"If it's because we're working together—"

"It's not just that." He braced his hands on the arms of the old-fashioned dining chair, and for a moment she thought he'd stay seated. But he didn't.

"Are you not attracted to me?"

"That's not it, and you know it." He pulled his wallet—a beat-up leather thing that was flat as a pancake—out of his back pocket and threw a few bills onto the table, waving her away when she reached for her own money.

"I'm not letting you foot the whole bill," she said.

"It's a work dinner. I'll expense it."

He waited for her to walk past and she did, awkwardly ambling between the tables with her backpack in front of her so she wouldn't accidentally bump anyone. The old Italian woman who'd brought their drinks earlier watched them leave, her hooded eyes unabashedly curious. Quinn made a point of not making eye contact with her. She didn't care what other people thought... and maybe if she repeated that mantra enough times it would stick.

"This place means something to you, doesn't it?" she said as they waited on the side of the road for a cab. "The restaurant, I mean."

"Yeah, I used to come here a lot as a kid. The people who own this place are practically family." He looked as if he was going to say something else, but he didn't.

When the cab pulled up, he held the door for her—the—perfect gentleman. She scooted across the back-seat and he climbed in next to her. He seemed to take up all the space, and the air around him vibrated.

"What's your family like?" Quinn asked, fiddling with the bag cradled in her lap.

He snorted. "Next question."

"That bad, huh?" When he didn't respond, she punched him lightly in the arm. "Come on, you told me about the thing with Logan. Why get all closed up now?"

The streetlights flickered over his face as the cab whisked them away from the restaurant. "My father's a control freak who was more concerned about his legacy at the FBI than about his son."

"I don't understand."

"After we found out that I couldn't maintain my position with the FBI police department because of my hearing, I wanted to take a break." He stared out the window, his eyes distant. "I wanted to give myself some time to plan my next move. To assess what my injury meant to all my career aspirations."

"But he didn't agree?"

"No. He had me shoved into a new position at the FBI as quickly as possible. He couldn't stand the thought that I might not follow in his precious footsteps." He let out a bitter laugh. "And God forbid that anyone might think the son of Graham Odell had a moment of weakness."

"How did he react when you decided to leave?"

"That argument could have woken the dead. He said I was being a quitter and I was being disloyal to the FBI and everything he'd done to help set me up there." He paused. "We haven't spoken much since."

"That's sad."

Aiden shrugged. "We didn't have the best relationship before this, so it's nothing new."

"Don't tell me that you don't want a relationship with him." She reached out and touched his thigh. "I won't believe that for a second."

"I do, but unfortunately that ship has sailed." He grabbed her hand and squeezed. "I'm not going to let it stop me from living my life."

Silence settled over them, and Quinn wondered if bringing Aiden home was actually a good idea—she didn't often have guests. Scratch that. She *never* had guests.

Even Alana didn't come around often. They usually went to her place to play games or watch movies because her couch wasn't in the same room as the bed, and you didn't have to climb over the coffee table slash footstool to get into the kitchen.

"So, did you grow up in Brooklyn?" she asked as the cab cruised through the streets.

The distant glow of Manhattan lit the night like a strange nighttime sun. It was hard not to notice how close Aiden's thigh was to hers on the seat, his magnetic power pouring out into the air around them, filling it with his masculinity.

"I actually live in the house I grew up in." The streetlights flashed against his face, making his cheekbones look sharper and his jaw more angled.

"Where?"

"Park Slope," he replied.

Of course he lives in the expensive part of town...

"I bet it's a beautiful house."

"It is." He nodded. "I'm lucky."

"How come you're not married?" she blurted out.

"Gee, you're full of questions tonight." He raised a brow.

"I mean it sounds like you come from money," she barreled on. "You've got a decent job, you're..."

"I'm what?" He smirked in the near darkness.

"You're attractive." She swallowed and hoped the heat in her cheeks wasn't showing. "Why no girl?"

"My work comes first." He slid a hand along the back of the seat until it rested behind but didn't touch her. "A lot of girls think it's a thrill to date a guy in the Bureau, but then they realize it can be dangerous. And it takes up a lot of my time and energy. Then once the thrill is gone they don't want me anymore. They want someone with a nine-to-five job, someone safe."

She bit down on her lip. "Safe isn't so bad, is it?"

"No. But it's not what I do. Sure, I'm not fighting a war. But we go up against some crazy, dangerous people...and sometimes they fight back. That kind of life isn't for everyone."

Her fingertips reached out to him, almost of their own accord, and she traced the shell of his ear. "Is that how this happened? The incident you told me about, did someone fight back?"

"Yeah." He covered her hand with his, pressing her

palm flat against his ear and turning his face so that his lips grazed her skin.

The air crackled between them, alive with the promise of what would happen if he came up to her apartment. Of what she *wanted* to happen...of what she was also *terrified* of happening.

Warmth flowed through her, making everything ache and throb. The way he looked at her—as though he'd burn her up—made her sex clench. He pulled her hand to his mouth and kissed the pads of her fingertips, his full lips soft and hot. Just a taste, and she was ready to climb into his lap and take what she needed.

Him. All of him.

Instead, she asked, "What happened?"

"Another agent and I were serving an arrest warrant. When the guy didn't answer the door we went in, tried to clear the place. But he was hiding in a cupboard with a gun. When I tried to talk him out, he took a shot at me. Close range." His face remained still as stone. "Luckily for me he was high as a fucking kite and he missed by a mile."

"He could have killed you?" A tremor ran through her, the gravity of his story swirling around in her head like sand kicked up by a gust of wind. "How can you be so calm when you talk about it?"

"Because he *didn't* kill me and I'm grateful for that every goddamn day." He pressed another kiss to the palm of her hand. "It sucks that my hearing is all messed up, but I'm still alive."

The cab pulled up beside her apartment building and she paid quickly, forcing the cash into the cabbie's hand before Aiden could try and "expense" it.

For some reason, knowing that he might have died

unleashed something inside her. A desire to live? Because she, too, could have been dead—or at least her attacker might not have been foiled at the last minute. She might not have been saved. But his outlook was logical, positive. He didn't live in fear of a gunman jumping out of a closet, so why should she?

Alone on the sidewalk, her quiet street had retired for the evening. Aiden stood next to the cab, the door still open and his arm resting on it.

"I should go," he said.

"Don't." She fisted her hands in his shirt and pressed her body against his.

The moment her hips bumped his and she felt the long, hard ridge of his erection against her belly, power flowed through her. She wanted him and she wasn't going to take no for an answer.

"Come upstairs." Her lips brushed his jaw. "I want to finish what we started the other night."

A moan escaped his lips and he ground his hips against hers. "Quinn, damn it…you're making this hard."

"So hard you're serving up that perfect double entendre without even realizing it?" Her teeth nipped at his neck, the muscles there corded and straining. "Come with me. I'll make it more than hard."

Aiden wrapped an arm around her waist and moved them out of the way of the cab, slamming the door shut behind him. "What do you want out of this?"

"Isn't it obvious?" She looped her arms around his neck and dragged his head down to hers.

She tasted beer on his breath as her lips moved over his, nudging his mouth open so her tongue could savor him. Her fingers tangled in the lengths of his hair, tugging and threading and gripping as she opened up to him.

"I want sex, Aiden. With you."

His lashes brushed her temple as he rested his cheek against hers. "We can't let this get in the way of working together."

"It won't, and believe me, I don't want anyone finding out."

His deft fingers skated up the length of her neck, his thumbs brushing her cheekbones as he held her head in place. "Neither do I."

"Then it's settled. You'll come upstairs, we'll enjoy one another's company and it'll be our little secret." She punctuated the last three words with feather-light kisses along his jaw. "It's our business anyway. No one else needs to know."

Anticipation skittered through her body, the promise of having him again lighting her up like the skyline at night. Glittering and vibrant.

"Why me?" he asked.

The question took her by surprise, and she covered it by grabbing his hand and pulling him toward the building. "What do you mean?"

"What you're doing now requires an amount of trust that you don't usually give people." He held the door for her. "Or am I wrong?"

They entered the building and headed up to her first-floor apartment, the sound of their footsteps echoing in the quiet stairwell. Somewhere in the distance Latin music played and a child cried. A TV show blared from her neighbor's door. It almost covered the sound of the neighbors fighting.

"It's just sex, Aiden. Why are you trying to read

more into it?" She avoided his eyes as she shoved the key into the lock, her hand trembling so that it took her a few goes to get it in properly.

"I want to make sure I don't end up on that list of guys who've hurt you." His hands settled on her hips, and his breath was hot against her ear. "I want to know what your boundaries are."

"Are you planning to do anything illegal to me?"

He shook his head. "No."

"Then we're good."

She pushed the door open and pulled him into her apartment. With one flick of a light switch the whole place was illuminated. Her tiny, cramped little home.

"Welcome to my *very* humble abode," she said as the door slammed shut behind them.

"Quinn." He came up behind her and wrapped his arms around her waist, resting his chin against her shoulder. "How about you drop the act for a minute and be straight with me."

"I am being straight." She bristled, but the gentle climb of his hand up and over her rib cage melted her bones, and she sagged back against him.

"So you'll be fine when we wake up together tomorrow morning?"

"Who says you're allowed to sleep over?" A smile curved on her mouth as he brushed her hair back and kissed the delicate space behind her ear.

"Who said we'd be sleeping?" He sucked on the soft bit of skin where her neck joined her shoulder, then he stilled. "But I do mean it. I want you to be okay tomorrow."

"You're worried I'm going to freak out again, aren't you?"

He spun her around and smoothed his hands over her shoulders and down her arms. "A little."

But I trust you.

The words danced around in her mind like mischievous sprites, kicking up all kinds of confusing emotions and sprinkling their crazy fairy dust all over her thoughts. With Aiden around, the world seemed to have fewer shadows, less darkness. Rose-colored glasses much?

Knowing he was friends with the boss added another complicated layer to their relationship. But tonight wasn't part of their assignment and it wouldn't interfere with her life at Cobalt & Dane. If there was one thing Quinn could do, it was separation. Who she was in the gaming world was totally different from who she was at work. Here, with him, she would be another person. One who embraced and enjoyed sex and wasn't afraid.

"If you do your job properly, I won't have the energy to freak out." She raised her eyebrow in challenge.

The concern in his face melted away. "You doubt my abilities in bed?"

"I don't doubt them, but I don't want you to slack off, either."

He picked her up, supporting her ass in the firm grip of his hands. Laughing, she wrapped her legs around him, locking her boots around his lower back and moaning at the hard press of him between her legs.

"I *don't* slack off...not when it comes to this," he growled. "We'll see who's ready to call it quits first."

"I'm an insomniac. I can stay up *all* night." Her teeth nipped at his earlobe.

"You slept pretty well last time." He carried her to the bed, sinking one knee into the mattress as she continued to cling to him like some kind of sex-starved barnacle. "You were purring like a kitten."

She *hadn't* slept that well in years…nor for a night since. "Beginner's luck."

"So tell me, Quinn, what game are we going to play tonight?" He laid her down on the bed and hovered over her. Not a single part of them touched, yet her whole body throbbed as if he was already on top of her.

"Hopefully, not a waiting game."

"You were the one who said we had all night." The corners of his eyes crinkled and he bent down, his hands on her boots.

Watching him unknot the laces was strangely erotic, as though he was slowly untangling the tension within her. Loosening her bonds. Freeing her.

He slipped the boots off one by one, revealing her neon-yellow-and-black Batman socks. Not exactly the attire of a practiced seductress. But soon they were gone, too, and he crawled up her body like a panther. Sleek and powerful.

Power wasn't normally something that attracted her. In fact, she often steered clear of men who had the kind of physical prowess that Aiden possessed. But instead of being intimidating, he wore it like a uniform. Something he would use to protect rather than control her.

"What's going on in that head of yours?" He braced himself with a hand on either side of her shoulders, hovering over her as he gently nudged her legs apart with his knees.

"Contemplating the secrets of the universe," she quipped.

"Then I'm not doing my job properly."

He lowered his hips to hers, pressing her into the

mattress. His hard thighs held her open while he shifted his weight to one hand and used the other to trace the outline of her body. Through the loose-knitted fabric of her sweater, she felt the heat of his palm.

The moment he touched her, all her erogenous zones screamed "me, me, me" at full volume. Her breasts ached and her nipples had already peaked into stiff buds before his fingers made it past her shoulder.

"Please," she murmured, arching her back to try and bring his hand closer to where she wanted it.

"*That's* more like it." A chuckle rumbled in the back of his throat as he placed kisses along the neckline of her sweater, taking his sweet damn time.

He skipped her breast altogether as his hand skated down her rib cage to the hem of her sweater, ducking under it so flesh met flesh as his palm pressed against her belly. Stroking his thumb back and forth, he waited.

"What's the holdup?" She propped herself up on her forearms.

"I've got an idea." His eyes sparkled like blue gemstones.

"What kind of idea?"

"A *sexy* idea." He sat up and looked around her room for a moment until his eyes locked on something.

Pushing up from her bed, he made it across her apartment in a few long-legged strides. When he returned, he had something in his hands. The belt of a silky bathrobe she'd bought at Comic Con a few years ago; the one that looked like a Stormtrooper uniform.

Panic sped through her veins and she sat up, tucking her knees to her chest. "You're *not* tying me up."

"No, I want you to tie *me* up." He held out the piece of silk, moving toward her slowly.

"Why?"

"Because it'll put you in full control. You can do whatever you like to me, however you like in whichever way you like it." His pupils were hungry and dark, drawing her toward him. "No need to freak out if you're the one in charge."

Her fingers brushed his hand as she took the length of silk from him, enjoying the sensual slip of it against her palms. Could she really take command? The idea buzzed in her head, a million sexy possibilities flying around.

"Are you doing this just for me?" she asked, absently wrapping the silk around her palm.

"I'm doing this for both of us. Having a beautiful woman string me up and take charge is unbelievably hot." The words came out gravelly and rough. "I want this."

He knelt on the edge of her bed, running his palms up and down his thighs. So close to where his erection strained against the fly of his jeans, long and hard. Her body pulsed with unexpected power. A tight ache gathered between her thighs at the thought of having him at her mercy.

Aiden wasn't weak; she knew that for sure. The way he'd taken charge in the office and on that first night, bringing her the kind of intense pleasure she'd never known before, showed he was totally comfortable in the driver's seat. But the idea of having all that strength and masculinity contained, bound and controlled…hell. Moisture gathered at her sex, need spiking hard and fast within her.

"Strip." The commanding tone in her voice was totally foreign to her, and for a moment she wondered where it had come from. This wasn't her. Quinn Dellinger was *not* a powerful person.

But he made her feel that way, and she wanted to revel in it.

"Yes, ma'am." With the lazy swagger of a cowboy, he pushed up from the bed.

"Slowly."

He smiled, clearly enjoying being told what to do. Shrugging out of his jacket, he tossed it to the floor with more theatrics than she'd expected. Then he ran his palms up and down his chest. Her breath caught in her throat as he snagged the hem of his T-shirt and pulled it up, revealing fair skin, ribbed with muscles. Everything bulged and flexed as he moved, but her eyes were drawn to the sharp V at his waist. Two lines pointing toward heaven. Those muscles were God's gift to the world; she was sure of it.

With a cheeky smile he threw the T-shirt at her and it landed on her head. Clearly, being turned on as all hell meant her reflexes had gone to sleep. Laughing, she pulled the shirt off and tossed it on top of his jacket.

"I feel like we should have some music for this," he said, wrenching at the buckle of his jeans. "Then I could get all Magic Mike on you."

"You don't need music, Aiden." She leaned forward on her knees so she could watch as he drew the zipper down with excruciating leisure.

"Is that a fact?" His thumbs tucked into the waistband of his jeans and he pushed them down, toeing off his shoes at the same time. His socks were gone in a flash.

Attempting to dull the ache in her sex—or perhaps to heighten it—she squeezed her thighs together and resisted the urge to touch herself. No other guy had ever managed to get her as excited as this. And they hadn't even gotten past first base.

"All of it," she breathed. "Off. Now."

"I'm glad you've taken to my idea." Without an ounce of modesty, he whipped off his black boxer briefs and stood in front of her. Hands by his side, awaiting her instruction.

His cock jutted forward, hard and strong and oh, so tempting. Unable to resist, she crawled to the edge of the bed and touched her tongue to his cock, catching a pearled bead of pre-cum from the tip of him. An anguished groan sounded out in the room.

She had him. Tonight he would be hers.

"Sit." She pointed to the bed and thanked her lucky stars she'd kept the ornate headboard her mother had picked up at the local thrift shop when she was a teenager.

Now, instead of stringing up pictures of long-haired rock stars and her favorite game characters, she would be tying up a man. Times had certainly changed.

Aiden did as he was asked, setting himself down on her bed and presenting his hands to her like a birthday present. A frisson of excitement charged through her nervous system, fueling her on. Filling her with confidence.

"Good boy," she murmured as she wrapped the silk around his wrists.

She'd never claimed to be a Girl Scout, so the knot was probably an abysmal attempt, but it would have to do. She lifted his arms up and secured him to the headboard, straddling his hips as she worked.

"Jesus, Quinn." He arched against her, the hard

length of him digging into her inner thigh. "You're so damn sexy."

"And you moan a lot when you're turned on." She put the finishing touch on her amateur bondage attempt and kissed him so hard his head pressed back against the bed frame. "I like it."

"And I like you." His eyes blazed for a moment before he squeezed them shut again when she wrapped her fingers around him. "Christ, I *love* that."

Hardness melded with softness as she stroked him, pumping her fist up and down. She twisted her hand with each stroke as he gasped and jerked his hips up to match her rhythm. Her other hand cupped his balls, kneading them and tugging them.

"Maybe we should have put some rules in place—" His words dissolved into a moan. "Rule number one, you can't make me come in the first five seconds."

"Negotiation time is over." She leaned forward, boldly whispering in his ear as she continued to pleasure him. "If I want you to come now, you'll come now."

Oh, my God! Who the hell was she?

11

AIDEN'S GAMBLE HAD most definitely paid off. Quinn straddled him, still fully clothed save for her feet, and she was a whole new person. A sexy, take-no-prisoners person. One who was going to give him the quickest orgasm of his life if he didn't do something about it right this second.

"We've got all night. There's no need to rush." His body had to work overtime to push enough blood to his head so he could form a sentence. No easy feat when she was working her magic hands up and down him.

"So stop me," she challenged him. "Untie your hands and *make* me."

For a moment he wanted to. He could easily wriggle loose of the poorly tied knot. But that wasn't the point. He'd given her the power, and taking it away now would undermine what he wanted to achieve. Instead he clenched his jaw and fought the rising tide of pleasure lapping at him, pulling him closer to release.

"That's what I thought." Her smug grin was reward enough for him, but then she shuffled farther down and dipped her head between his legs.

"Uhhhh!" His body jerked hard when she wrapped her lips around the aching head of his cock. "That's not fair."

An evil laugh reverberated against him as she sucked him, drawing her mouth up and down his length with deliberate slowness. The second she sucked hard on his head he thought it was all over. But she pulled back at the last second, releasing him. Leaving him panting and perfectly frustrated.

"Maybe I should be in charge more often?" Untangling her limbs from the duvet, she stood and peeled her sweater off to reveal a highlighter-yellow bra.

"You *definitely* should be in charge more often."

The pink ends of her hair scattered around her shoulders, and she tugged out the little skull and crossbones clip by her ear. It pinged as it hit the nightstand. The dark eyeliner she'd worn that day had smudged, making her hazel eyes seem even bigger and brighter.

"Has anyone ever told you how goddamn sexy you are?" He rolled his shoulders as best he could with them tied above his head, fighting the urge to break free and grab her. Toss her onto the bed and worship her.

She swayed her hips as she reached behind her back to unclip her bra. "Just you."

"Bullshit."

Two perfect, pale breasts bobbed in front of his face as she ditched her bra. Her nipples were stiff and pink as roses. He ached to take one between his lips and roll his tongue over it.

She tossed aside her jeans and finally her panties, leaving her body bare for his eyes to feast on. Every part of her was beautiful, from her trim hips to her bony elbows, to the gentle curve of her calves and the sweet pinkness of her sex. He wanted it all.

"It's not bullshit." Her confidence faltered. "You're the only guy who's ever said it before."

"Well, that is a crime." How had anyone not appreciated how lucky he was to be with Quinn? Idiots. "Come here so I can make up for the stupidity of my gender."

She crawled onto his lap, her small thighs barely holding him down as he pushed against her. The tip of his cock grazed her sex; she was so wet. So hot.

"Condom?" He muttered through clenched teeth.

Reaching over, she dug around in the drawer next to the bed for what felt like hours, eventually holding a foil packet up triumphantly. The sound of it ripping only heightened his excitement, and when she placed it at the tip of him, rolling it down slowly, he thought he might burst.

"Are you ready?" she asked, her lips pressing against his, her tongue gently sliding into his mouth.

"If I was any more ready it'd be over."

Pressing her hands into the center of his chest, she lifted her hips up and positioned him at her sex. His body screamed out for her, the chant of *yes, yes, yes* thundering in time with his pulse. The moment she slid down onto him the world shifted. Heat enveloped him like a tight fist, her muscles clenching and sucking him in deep.

"Aiden," she sighed, her head rolling back as she gripped the headboard and circled her hips. "You feel so good inside me."

What was sexier? The way her eyelids fluttered as she rocked up and down on his cock or the breathy, gravelly way she spoke to him? He had no idea.

"How good?"

Those dark smudgy eyes opened and a wicked smile curved on her lips. "Next time we do this, I'm going to gag you."

"Next time?" Lord, he never assumed he'd be that lucky.

She rocked her hips, her tiny breasts bouncing in front of his face. Straining against the silk, he rose up and caught one with his mouth. He rolled the hard nipple over his tongue and suckled. Her skin was creamy, soft. Sweet. Like silky ice cream.

"I'm so close," she gasped, the words tumbling out in garbled pleasure. "Aiden, I'm... I'm..."

She shifted, changing the angle so she could brush her clit against his pubic bone with each stroke. Perspiration glowed on her skin, the scent of her arousal filling his nostrils. He blanked out everything but them and the amazing sensation of her riding him.

"I want to feel you, Quinn. I want to feel you come."

Her beautiful face scrunched up and she dipped a hand between her legs. As her fingers circled her sweet spot, spasms ran through her to him.

A high-pitched cry hit the air and she gasped his name, sending him over the edge. His thighs shook and his blood roared in his ears. Nothing had ever felt like that before. Nothing.

QUINN HAD NO idea how long she'd been slumped against Aiden's chest. Eventually he shifted, trying to stretch his muscles, and she realized he was still tied up.

"Want me to get that?" Her hands skated over his shoulders as she planted a kiss on his forehead.

"If you wouldn't mind."

Would pulling the silk from his wrists send her back into a spiral of fear and doubt? She toyed with the knot, biting down on the inside of her cheek. Moments ago she'd felt as powerful as a god, commanding their pleasure as though she'd never mistrusted the opposite sex.

As for Aiden…well, no one she'd ever been with came close to him. In *any* aspect.

"There you go." She pulled the silk tie through the ornate design on the headboard. He reached around her back, stroking the length of her spine as he held her close.

"That was incredible." His hot breath fanned her neck as he nibbled there. "*You're* incredible. You need to be in charge of all of the things."

She laughed. "I'm glad you have so much faith in me."

"I do."

Light danced in his eyes, his irises as blue as the sky on a calm summer day. Warm, inviting. Peaceful.

She waited for the nerves to come, for the thumping of her heartbeat or the twitch in her fingers. But her body felt like liquid pleasure, high on endorphins. Comfortable.

Safe.

As if sensing her confusion, he brushed the hair from her face and cupped her head. "All good?"

She nodded. "Yeah."

"Let me freshen up, okay?" He set her down on the bed and disappeared into her bathroom.

What would happen now? Would he leave? He had said something about being up all night.

Leaning over the edge of the bed, she reached around for something to wear and spotted his T-shirt. She lifted it up to her face and inhaled the scent of him—a hint of cologne, not too much, not too little. And something earthy, masculine.

Slipping the shirt over her head, she pushed up from the bed and grabbed a fresh pair of underwear from her drawer.

"Looks good on you," he said as he walked across her apartment, totally naked. "But what am I going to wear?"

"The birthday suit fits you pretty well."

He reached out to her and she stepped into his arms, but instead of hugging her he picked her up and carried her to the couch.

"Hey! What the hell?"

"It's game time." He set her down and retrieved his underwear. "We need to settle this once and for all."

"What?"

"'Mario Kart.' I'm going to whip your ass so you'll stop holding it over me."

A happy bubble formed inside her chest. "The hell you are. Prepare to eat shell!"

"Oh, it's on." A wide grin split across his face as he winked. "You're going down, Princess Peach."

"Screw that. I'm Yoshi or we're not playing."

A few hours later—and after kicking his ass enough times that he couldn't call it a fluke—Quinn set her Nintendo controller onto the couch beside her, triumphant. Never before had she felt so comfortable with a guy, so at ease. Sitting there in his T-shirt, inhaling his scent and absorbing the warmth of his thigh pressed against hers, she was unafraid.

"I admit defeat." He laughed and ditched his controller onto the floor before grabbing her around the waist and pulling her into his lap.

"I told you so." Her arms wound around him and she shrieked when he nuzzled her neck with his rough, stubbled chin.

"Yes, I bow to the 'Mario Kart' master." His nuzzling turned into something hotter as his tongue swiped her skin, his lips sucking at her. "Ready to claim your prize?"

"And what prize is that?"

"Me, kneeling at your feet in the shower." His hand slipped under the T-shirt and smoothed over her rib cage.

A sharp flare of pleasure ran through her when he tweaked her nipple and she gasped. "Do I get to tie you up again?"

"I'm going to use my hands this time." Standing, he picked her up easily and her thighs squeezed against his waist, her feet locking behind his lower back.

Her hand brushed over the light switch as they entered her tiny bathroom. There was barely enough space for both of them to stand, so he sat her down on the sink while he got the water running in the shower. He moved about the space as though he'd been there a thousand times before, and he looked as if he belonged. With her.

Don't tell me one orgasm and a "Mario Kart" win is enough to make you want to do the relationship thing?

Aiden's laugh brought her back into the present. "I dig the T-Rex shower curtain."

"That was a gift from Alana." The white shower curtain had a large decal of a black T-Rex wearing a floral shower cap and holding a scrubbing brush. "Part of my housewarming present. She couldn't stand the thought of me using the old one my mother had given me."

"She looks out for you, doesn't she?" Steam billowed out from the shower, and he held his arm under the spray to test the temperature.

"Yeah. We're a good team. She's one of the only people I trust in the whole world."

"Why's that?"

She shrugged. "Alana's never lied to me. Sometimes she'll tell me the things I don't want to hear, but I know everything out of her mouth is the truth, positive or not."

In one step he closed the gap between them, nudging her legs apart, his mouth descending on hers. It took her by surprise that he could still be so hungry for her after what they'd done. But he was hard against her, rigid and ready.

"You're insatiable," she said between kisses.

"And you're the best damn dessert a guy could ask for." He helped her down from the sink and steered her toward the shower. "Now it's prize time."

A shudder racked her body, the promise of him on his knees before her more than enough to start up a deep, cavernous ache in her sex. She wasn't done with him, not yet.

Warm water hit her skin as she stepped into the tub, the steam fogging up the air around them. But Aiden knew exactly what he was doing. He turned her around so she faced the tile, and a moment later something cool hit her shoulder. The scent of strawberries filled the air, and he used her shower puff to massage her back, working the liquid soap into her skin in sweeping circles.

"Now *this* is a good prize," she said, sighing and rolling her head.

"Just you wait." He moved the puff around her body, circling her butt cheeks and massaging the delicate skin of her inner thighs.

He covered every inch of her, reaching around to work up a lather over her breasts and stomach. Meanwhile he pressed against her from behind, the hard ridge of his cock fitting against her ass. After they'd rinsed the soap away, he turned her around and pressed her up against the wall. The shocking contrast of cool tiles against her back and warm water against her front made her jolt.

But the second he was on his knees there was nothing else. Hooking one of her legs over his shoulder, he opened her. She braced her hands against the tile but there was nothing to grip onto. Nothing to keep her safe.

"Hang on to me. I don't want you to fall." He pulled her hand to his head and she threaded her fingers through his lush curls, tugging involuntarily when he pressed his mouth against her sex.

Hesitation was not in his vocabulary. Rubbing her lips with his thumbs, he parted them and ran his tongue up the seam of her. It was all she could do to stay upright.

"You taste so sweet." His voice was almost drowned by the rush of water from the shower head and the drumming of her heartbeat in her ears. "I could do this for hours."

"I'm not going to last for hours. I—" A gasp wrenched from deep inside her cut off the words as he drew her clit between his lips.

He knew exactly what pressure she needed, not too much and not too little. He was the goddamn Goldilocks of giving head.

"Yes, Quinn?" Raising his eyes to look at her for a moment, he grinned. Clearly, he was enjoying having her at his mercy, even though he was the one on his knees.

"Back to work." She pushed his head down again, and his laugh reverberated against her thigh.

His hand bit into her ass as he held her against his face, the other teased her entrance. He promised pleasure but held back as he let his tongue do the work, drawing out her anticipation. Her muscles clenched as if trying to draw him in. When he finally pressed a finger inside her, it was all over. Wave after wave of release shuddered through her body, knocking her knees out from under her.

The taps squeaked as he shut the water off, still holding her upright with his other hand. Cool air hit her wet skin, and he wrapped a towel around her shoulders, tucking her under his arm.

"I'm not even going to ask how you got so good at that," she mumbled, her head still deliciously foggy.

"It's all about reading people. Sex is no different than having a conversation. I watch your body language so I can figure out what you like and what you don't like." His large hands rubbed circles over her back and arms, drying her off and returning the blood back into the rest of her body.

"And what do you think I like?"

"Me," he said with a cheeky grin. "My tongue, my fingers, my…"

Emboldened, she reached down and wrapped her fingers around his cock. "This, too."

"And I like seeing you so confident." He kissed the tip of her nose. "That's damn sexy."

BY THE TIME they'd made it back to the bed, Quinn had taken her newfound self-assurance and run with it. He'd lost himself in her again and again until the little clock on her bedside table flashed an obscene hour at them.

She lay curled up in his arms in the dark room, the glow of the streetlights filtering in through the cheap slatted blinds. Her head rested on his chest while she traced small circles around his nipple with one fingertip. Pink hair spilled across his stomach and he twirled it around his pointer finger.

"Thanks for giving me a chance to take over," she said. Her voice was small. Shy. As though they hadn't just been having the most passionate sex of his life.

"No thanks needed."

"I'm glad we met that night…despite the bumpy start."

"Me, too.

Her lashes brushed his chest as she blinked. "I know my fixation with honesty might seem strange but…it's important to me. I haven't been in a relationship for a long time because I find it hard to trust people." Each word sounded as though it had been forced out, as if she wanted to tell him but her body was resisting.

"You don't have to explain anything to me, Quinn."

"I want to. I want you to understand why I am the way I am." She shifted onto her stomach so she could look him in the eye. "I trusted a guy once. I thought he loved me."

He had an idea where this story was going, and he already hated this guy with a fierce passion. It was totally irrational, possibly unhinged. But he had no qualms about finding this guy and teaching him a lesson.

"What happened?" The tremble in his hands as

stroked her hair belied the calmness he'd forced into his voice.

"He filmed us." She buried her face into his shoulder. "Having sex. He set up a webcam and didn't tell me. And he sent the video feed to all his friends."

Flames licked at him. What kind of son of a bitch did something like that? She must have felt so violated. He gritted his teeth to stop himself from roaring in her defense.

"Then…" She hiccupped. "One of his friends turned up at my work. He said he'd send the recording to my mom if I didn't sleep with him. He tried to force me… but my boss found us before it got too far."

Shudders racked her small frame, and he hugged her so tight he thought he might break her in two. "No one will ever do that to you again. Do you hear me?"

Wetness spread over his skin as she cried. No wonder she'd been prickly as hell. Who could possibly trust another human being after that? He didn't want to imagine her terror because it would be the end of him.

But he would keep his word. For as long as Quinn would have him around, he would not let anything happen to her.

12

Over the course of the next week, Quinn and Aiden fell into a routine. They'd work at Third Planet Studios during the day, leave separately and meet at Gustoso for dinner. Then they'd go back to her place and spend the night pleasuring one another.

Zach had given her a few sullen looks when she rolled into work late, but otherwise he'd behaved himself and no one else seemed to care. But she and Aiden had made no further progress on the assignment, and today they had to face the music with Rhys. *Very early.*

Quinn couldn't remember the last time she'd voluntarily arrived at work at 7:30 a.m. Scratch that; she couldn't remember the last time she'd been voluntarily *awake* that early. But after another glorious night with Aiden, her body was singing like a bluebird in a children's cartoon.

Her footsteps matched Aiden's as they walked through the lobby of the Cobalt & Dane offices. They were meeting Rhys to get him up to speed on their first two weeks at Third Planet Studios now that Aiden had completed the follow-up from the staff interviews.

The elevator dinged at their floor and Quinn stepped out first, almost walking straight into Owen.

"I see hell has officially frozen over...unless my watch has stopped and it's actually ten o'clock." He leaned against the reception desk, a cocky grin on his face.

"I have a meeting." She brought the giant coffee cup to her lips.

Aiden nodded at Owen and walked past them as if he hadn't been entering the office with Quinn. He didn't even look back or give her a signal that they would catch up later.

Hang on, you both agreed to keep it on the down low. Don't go getting pissed because he's sticking to the script.

"Does he have a meeting, too?" Owen's lips spread into a cheeky grin, a blond brow arching as he waited for her response.

"Probably. We *are* working on the same assignment." Her attempt at indifference failed hard when heat crawled up her cheeks. And Owen, damn him, didn't miss a thing.

"Just a coincidence that you both got coffee from Valentina's?" His eyes tracked every minuscule movement on her face.

There were definite downsides to working with a bunch of ex-cops. Keeping a secret was hard, and evasion wasn't nearly as effective on them as it was on other people.

"I like Valentina's. They don't charge for a shot of vanilla." She sipped again and shrugged.

"Yeah, and it's a good five blocks out of the way. Precious time for a girl who needs her sleep, especially when you could have gone downstairs to the Brunswick Café if you wanted a free shot of vanilla." He folded his arms across his chest, smugness radiating from his every pore. "Like you usually do."

"What's with the Spanish Inquisition?" she snapped. "I wanted a coffee and we walked to work together. Not exactly worthy of a headline."

Even her carefully worded responses couldn't outmaneuver Owen's dogged curiosity. Once he set his sights on something there was no stopping him.

But she had to try, because having the office know she'd slept with the boss's best friend was *not* part of her career plan.

"Did you bump into him before or after you decided to go to Valentina's?"

"Before," she said through gritted teeth. He had her backed into a corner, and the only thing she could do now was keep her mouth shut.

"Did you bump into him last night, too?"

"Back off." Her hand tightened around the coffee cup and the lid popped off from the pressure. Thankfully, she'd drunk enough that the liquid didn't spill over the edge. "Look what you made me do!"

He bent down and retrieved her lid, handing it to her before laying a hand on her shoulder. "Nothing to be ashamed of, Quinn. I'm happy for you—he's a real-life guy. Not some 'World of Warcraft' dark elf bullshit."

"I don't pick up guys on 'World of Warcraft.'" The steam coming out of her ears could have powered a train. "Not that it's any of your business."

"I won't tell. Promise." He sauntered off and threw her a mischievous grin over one shoulder.

Owen was a damn gossip, and she had no idea if she

could trust him to keep it quiet. But he hadn't spilled the beans when their friend Max had fallen for a client, so maybe he'd stay true to his word.

She'd have to steer totally clear of Aiden while they were at work from now on. The last thing she needed was anyone else figuring out what they'd gotten up to.

When she got that promotion, it *wouldn't* be because she'd slept her way there. Maybe this was the reminder she needed to get her eye back on the prize. Her feelings for Aiden didn't matter here, and she couldn't let them interfere with her goal.

"Hey, Quinn." Rhys came up beside her, his satchel slung over one shoulder. "Ready for our meeting?"

"Sure am," she replied as she fell into step beside him.

They reached his office door, and she hovered as he dug the key out of his bag. "Hey, can I ask you a question?" she said.

He held the door open and ushered her inside. "What is it?"

"I was wondering…" Her fingers traced the waffle-cut design on the coffee cup's heat-protection sleeve. "Was there any other reason I didn't get the job than lack of experience?"

Surely Rhys would have known about Aiden's connection to Logan. Would he tell her the truth?

"What makes you ask that?" He detached his laptop from the docking station on his desk and stacked two manila folders on top of it.

"I guess I want to go a long way here and I need to know if there's anything else standing in my way."

"Quinn, you're smart and capable. I have no doubt you'll do great things with your career."

"But?"

"Some hiring decisions aren't about that."

"What do you mean?"

"There are rules that we have to follow with Human Resources. Sometimes we advertise a position that we already have a preferred candidate for." He rubbed at the back of his neck. "Logan requested Aiden for that position and, objectively, he was the best candidate for the role. So we hired him."

"Was that before or after I interviewed for the job?"

Rhys's dark eyes narrowed. "Before. But we interview each candidate with the intention of assessing their suitability. I still wanted to give you the chance to show you're interested in moving up. It's a good thing, Quinn, even if we weren't able to give you a job right away."

"But you knew I wouldn't match up to him."

"I knew you didn't have the same experience. But you got a spot on this assignment because of it." They stepped out into the hallway and Rhys shut the door behind them. "Look, Logan and Aiden are friends. I didn't have much say in the matter."

She followed him toward the meeting room. "I get it."

His nose crinkled and he lowered his voice. "It's a hard lesson to learn, but some people use their connections to get through life. Personally, I prefer hard work to get to the top. But then again, maybe I'm old-fashioned."

The way he said it made her stomach churn. It was clear he didn't appreciate being forced to hire Aiden— despite admitting that the other man *did* have the skill-set for the job. How would he feel if he found out she was sleeping with Aiden? Would he think that was her way of using who she knew to get to the top?

"He seems to be doing a good job so far," she said, wanting to defend him.

"I have no doubt." Rhys patted her on the shoulder. "But I'm sure when you get to where you want to be, it'll be because you made it there on your own steam. And I'll be proud of you for that."

She nodded, forcing a tight smile across her lips. If she wanted that promotion, she'd need to make *damn* sure that no word of her and Aiden's extracurricular activities made it to the team. There was no way in hell she'd let anyone question whether or not she deserved to be promoted.

AIDEN FELT AS if he'd been dodging land mines ever since he arrived at the office. First the knowing smirk from Owen Fletcher in the reception area. Then Jin had dropped Logan's name casually into conversation in a way that made him suspect their friendship wasn't a secret. Now the Third Planet meeting was about to start, and Quinn was studiously ignoring him.

Needless to say, their happy post-sex bubble had been well and truly burst.

"Thanks for coming, guys," Rhys said as they all took a seat at the table. "How's the assignment progressing so far?"

Aiden opened his mouth to start going through the report he'd prepared, but Quinn beat him to it.

"We have one employee exhibiting suspicious behavior. A few days ago I overheard him on the phone talking to someone about confidential information." She squared her small shoulders.

"What confidential information?" Rhys asked, dropping down into the chair at the head of the table.

"We don't know yet. He seemed hesitant to provide it to whoever was on the line because of Aiden." Her gaze flicked across the table to him but didn't linger. "Then he said he would get it…whatever *it* is."

"That could be information about the design engine." Rhys paused his typing and scratched his head.

"Yes." She bobbed her head. "There's something else. One of the staff members has been harassing female employees."

Rhys raised an eyebrow. "Has he been harassing you?"

"Uh…" Her lower lip sank under the weight of her teeth. "Kind of."

He blew out a breath. "Yes or no, Quinn?"

"No." Her gaze dropped to the table's surface where she idly tapped her fingers in an erratic beat. "Not exactly."

"Why did you bring it up then?"

"Well, we should do something about it. One of the other junior designers came to me and said he'd been giving her a hard time. .He made an intern leave. She filed a complaint against him but she dropped it because he threatened her." Quinn blew a strand of hair out of her eyes. "He's Walt's nephew. We can't ignore that."

"Sexual harassment is outside the scope of this assignment." Rhys looked up from his computer. "Bring me something to tie him to the information leaks and then we'll investigate further."

A bright flush spread out over her cheeks at the boss's reprimand. She glanced at Aiden as if to ask him to step in and support her concerns. But Rhys was right; this wasn't part of the assignment. However, he'd definitely be keeping an eye on Zachary J. Levitt, that was for sure. Slimy bastard wouldn't lay a hand on Quinn, assignment or no assignment.

"How have the interviews wrapped up?" Rhys's tone confirmed the harassment discussion was over. "Did you talk to the guy on the phone person? Tell me we have a name."

"Christopher Mayer. He's been with the company two years, recently promoted to game designer. His record is clean other than one disciplinary infraction for emailing sensitive information…hence why he was on my list for the first round of interviews." His fingers toyed with the edge of the notes he'd prepared before leaving Third Planet yesterday. "I followed up again with him this week, and he claims he was sending work to his home computer. The email log supports that. It was only a scope document for a new project, Galactic Warrior. The email did not contain any financials or code. No reference to the engine, either."

"How long ago did that happen?"

"About three months."

Across the table Quinn paled noticeably. Where bright pink had dotted her cheeks before, now there was nothing by a pallid wash of white.

"You okay?" he asked.

"Yeah." She pressed a hand to her stomach. "Maybe too much coffee."

The sound of Rhys's fingers flying across the keys of his laptop filled the silence.

Something was definitely up with Quinn. First she'd jumped over him to have the first say in this meeting, despite knowing he was in charge of the assignment. Now she looked as if she'd seen a ghost.

"Dig up what you can on Mayer and check into the

guy who's been harassing staff," Rhys said. "I don't want us to take our eye off the prize, but if this guy is shady in one area, he might be shady in others."

"Got it." Aiden nodded.

Rhys packed up his computer and was out of the room before Quinn had moved a muscle. She could have passed for one of those statue-impersonation street performers.

"Earth to Quinn." He waved a hand in front of her face. "Want to share a cab to Third Planet?"

"No." The word seemed to come out without her lips moving, and then all of a sudden the spell was broken. Her eyes darted around the room and her tongue swiped along her lower lip. "I uhh… I'm going to walk, actually. I need to clear my head."

"Okay." He pushed up from his chair and rolled it back under the desk. "This doesn't have anything to do with Owen catching us coming out of the elevator together, does it?"

"What?" Her face was vacant for a moment, then she blinked. "No, it's not that."

"Then what's wrong? You spaced out."

"It's nothing. We agreed to keep things professional in the office, didn't we?"

That was true, but it was hard to keep things professional when every time she walked past him the scent of strawberry shower gel assaulted his senses. The memory of it foaming on her skin while he rubbed her down wouldn't leave his brain.

"Yeah, we did." He tried to subtly adjust the front of his pants so she wouldn't see that all she had to do was come within three feet of him to give him a raging hard-on.

"Good." Her fingers thrust up into her hair, pushing the long strands out of her face. She'd left it down today after they'd showered, and it flowed around her shoulders like pink-and-brown silk. "Anyway, I'll see you later."

She took off before he had the chance to ask any more questions. A bad feeling roiled in his gut. Something from that meeting had freaked her out, and he was going to find out what it was.

13

Shit, shit, *shit!*

Quinn grabbed her backpack and hurried out of the office. The problems were piling up, and her frayed nerves were settling in for the long haul. Owen knew she'd slept with Aiden, and after chatting with Rhys it was clear that she'd be *persona non grata* if he found out about it.

But she'd have to deal with that later. Right now she had to figure out if Hawaiian shirt guy—aka Christopher—was leaking information to Alana. Her best friend. A person she trusted.

Alana had gone to the cocktail party to speak to someone from Third Planet Studios. She'd even admitted that a couple of months ago she'd gotten a "sneak peek" at the plans for their latest "Galactic Warrior" game. Quinn had assumed she meant an early press release, not confidential information accessed via an inside person. But the timing and the content of the email Aiden had found pointed to a different conclusion.

She jabbed at the elevator call button and sagged in relief when the doors opened immediately. Fingers trembling, she hesitated for a moment before dialing Alana's number.

"Quinn? How are you? I thought you'd dropped off the face of the earth. WoW is *not* the same without you."

The elevator doors pinged and she hurried toward the exit, desperate to put some space between her and work. "Have you been stealing information from Third Planet Studios?"

The pause seemed to drag on forever.

"Excuse me?" Alana eventually laughed on the other end of the line, though it sounded a little forced. "I haven't stolen anything."

"Be straight with me," she pleaded. "Are you or are you not getting access to confidential information at Third Planet Studios?"

Outside the weather was ironically beautiful. The cool temperatures had been broken by a glowing sun, and a warm breeze trickled across her skin as a bird chirped. A fucking *bird*.

Too bad there was a dark, thunderous cloud hanging over her head.

A clicking noise in the background told her Alana was tapping her nails against something. "This doesn't sound like a personal question, Quinn. Why are you asking me this?"

"Because my boss gave me a second chance at that promotion."

"That's fantastic—"

"My assignment is to investigate an information leak for Third Planet Studios."

Pause. "Oh."

"Yeah." A dull pain thudded behind her eyes as she walked along Broadway, dodging a fancily dressed woman coming out of Bloomingdale's with an expensive purse tucked under her arm. "What do you know about it?"

"Not a lot." She took a deep breath. "I've been getting information from this guy for a while, but he got spooked a few months back because someone caught him emailing stuff out of the company."

"What's his name?" She knew, but hearing Alana say it would mean that there was still some trust left between them.

The silence dragged on until a sigh sounded on the other end of the line and Alana finally said, "Christopher."

"What information has he been sending you?"

Bloomingdale's blurred past as she stormed ahead. People moved out of her way as soon as they caught her expression. The Third Planet building was close by and she needed a plan. ASAP.

"Documents with their plans for future games." A note of hesitation in her voice made Quinn's ears prick.

"What else?"

"There's this guy who works there and he's been victimizing female staff. The company does *nothing* about it because he's related to the owner." Her voice wobbled. "It's bullshit, Quinn. The industry does not need people like that. He basically attacked my friend Sarah."

"She was an intern there?" The pieces clicked into place.

"Yeah, she made a complaint and he threatened to come after her. How did you know?"

"But you never received information about the game design engine, right?"

"What are you talking about? I don't know anything about a game design engine."

Quinn believed her. Alana wasn't in the business of trading corporate information. She wasn't playing spies and profiting off trade secrets.

She wanted to change the industry to make it safer for women. That was all she cared about.

"The leak I'm investigating is around the engine, not this thing with Zach Levitt."

"So you *do* know who I'm talking about. He's a predator, Quinn. Tell me you don't have anything to do with him. He scared Sarah so bad—"

"I can imagine." Quinn came to a stop at the entrance to the Third Planet building and looked up the tall, reflective column. "But what does he have to do with the game design documents?"

"Nothing, directly. But I've been searching for a way to take Third Planet down for a while. The stuff about Walt's nephew never seems to stick, though." She sighed. "So I got creative. If I can't get Walt for sexist work practices then I'll expose him for sexist game designs. If enough people boycott the company maybe he'll change his ways."

"Tell me you didn't do anything illegal to get this information."

Silence.

"Alana." She ground the heel of her hand against her eye to quell the throbbing. "What did you do?"

"I might have gotten access to Christopher's email and found out that he was cheating on his wife…and blackmailed him a little."

"And how did you get access to his email?" She shook her head. "Wait. Actually, I don't want to know."

"Please, Quinn. We won't ever be able to change things unless people like Zachary and Walt are taken down." She clucked her tongue. "So maybe my methods weren't one hundred percent ethical, but it's for the greater good."

"Why didn't you tell me about any of this?"

"I didn't want you to be ashamed of me."

How could this have gotten so messy so quickly? There was no way Aiden would back off on Alana's informant if she brought it to his and Rhys's attention. But if she didn't, it could be her job. Shit.

"I'm not ashamed of you, Alana. I just…did you have to blackmail him? That's a fucking crime."

"It's his word against mine. They can't prove anything." She drew a shaky breath.

"You'd better hope not."

"Please don't let them go after Christopher. He'll fold quicker than a shitty poker hand. All I wanted was enough evidence to do an exposé on Third Planet. They can't keep covering up this kind of behavior. Sarah *still* hasn't been able to find work because she's terrified it'll happen again."

Quinn wanted to be angry. No, scratch that. She wanted to be *furious*.

But she thought of Sarah, this girl she'd never met—probably never would meet—and how frightened she must be. Quinn understood that feeling all too well.

She sighed. "I can't make any promises. But I'll do my best. Just stop talking to this guy."

Her best friend had done something monumentally stupid. But Alana had been there for Quinn when she'd needed someone, and in a way this was also her way of being there for Sarah. Quinn had to help them both.

As for Aiden…well, she had no idea whether or not she could trust him with this. His job was everything to him. What if he wanted to throw Alana under the bus to get his *runs on the board*?

She couldn't risk it. She'd have to fix this situation on her own.

AIDEN ALWAYS RELIED on his instinct. He didn't act on it without proof, but he listened to it nonetheless. And today it was screaming loud and clear: warning, shit-storm ahead.

Logan had caught him on the way out and suggested they walk together since he was off to a client meeting in the same direction. The last thing Aiden had wanted was company, but he'd barely seen Logan since he started. The guy was busy with a capital B. No one worked as hard on their business as he did. It was part of the reason Aiden wanted to work for him. Success was catching, and Logan had it in abundance.

"How are you settling in?" Logan asked as they crossed an intersection. "Sorry I haven't been able to catch up with you until now."

"You know me. I don't need a babysitter."

Logan slapped him on the back. "I know. But I begged you to come and work for me so I didn't want you to think it was all talk. I have big plans for you."

The words echoed in his head. It was exactly what Rhys had said. Big plans. "Hey, can I ask you something?"

"Sure."

"Does everyone know you brought me across?"

Logan raised an eyebrow and ran a hand along the edge of his stubble-coated jaw. "I shared your experience with Rhys and our office manager, Addison, before you came in for an interview. I wasn't planning on keeping it a secret."

"Right."

"Worried that people will walk on eggshells around you?"

He laughed. "Nothing gets past you, does it?"

"I'm not running a security company because of my good looks." The creases around his eyes deepened as he smiled. "But I won't hesitate to back you if anyone tries to say you weren't the best damn candidate for the job."

"Even over one of your own staff members?"

"Are you talking about Quinn? She's smart and I want to see her succeed, but this wasn't her time." They rounded a corner, sidestepping a woman with a stroller. "You need to stop worrying so much about other people thinking you're worthy. I don't care that you're my best friend. If you were a Muppet I wouldn't have hired you. And I'd tell you that to your face."

He didn't doubt it. Logan was known for being blunt to the nth degree; he had a short fuse and an even shorter attention span. He'd burned through a lot of employees when he'd first taken over the reins at Cobalt & Dane. Weeding out the deadwood, he'd called it. Then he'd filled the gaps with guys like him—dedicated, hard-working. Loyal.

Aiden was honored to be counted as one of them. "She's got more potential that you give her credit for."

"Don't tell me she's gotten under your skin?"

"She can do more than fixing printers and screwing in lightbulbs."

"Screwing in lightbulbs?"

"You know what I mean. Mundane crap. You could hire a monkey to do that."

Logan snorted. "What you do on your personal time is your business. But you keep it out of the office, okay? And leave running my business to me."

That was as close as he would get to having Logan's blessing. But it was enough for him.

"I'm just saying, you have talented staff. If you don't utilize them, they'll leave."

Logan gave him a look that said the conversation was over. "How's your brother doing? I heard he split up with his wife. That really blows."

"Yeah, Marcus is pretty cut up about it."

"I'm sorry to hear that." His face softened. "Maybe we should take him out for a drink, or is he doing his usual withdrawal thing?"

"He stopped by my place two weeks ago, but he didn't want to talk about the separation."

"Like father, like son." Logan shook his head. "You're an unemotional lot, you Odells."

"You can talk." Aiden moved to sock him in the arm but Logan dodged the blow easily.

"I don't put myself in a position where I need to get emotional." He tapped the side of his head and winked. "See, I'm smart like that."

Aiden slowed his pace and they came to a stop in front of the coffee shop a few doors down from Third Planet Studios. He needed caffeine before he could face Quinn.

"Okay, big guy." Logan slapped his palm on Aiden's back. "I just wanted to say I'm glad you saw the light and decided to come and work with me. And let's take Marcus out soon, okay?"

"Absolutely."

Ten minutes later Aiden walked into the Third Planet Studios office with a coffee in one hand. He'd wanted to buy one for Quinn, the order had hovered on the tip of his tongue, but it would draw unnecessary attention to them. Still, he felt the need to make some kind of connection with her. Talk to her. Something to put his mind at ease after she'd shot out of their meeting like a rocket.

"You're back," Joan said, falling into step beside him. "What's the plan for today?"

"Just a few follow-up questions."

"Well, your meeting room is set up. I wasn't sure what time you were coming in so I haven't booked anyone in to see you. But if you want me to sit in on any meetings, I'll be free in the next hour."

"Thanks. Do you have those access card reports I requested?"

"Of course. Come to my office and I'll give them to you now." She bustled ahead, a stack of folders under one arm. "Whatever you need."

Quinn wasn't at her desk when he walked past. Her desk looked untouched, too neat. Given the state of her apartment, he wouldn't say she was a messy person, by any stretch…but she wasn't exactly meticulous, either. He paused.

Her laptop screen was locked, the background set to a page displaying "Galactic Warrior" fan art. The cursor flashed in the field where her password would be typed.

There weren't any papers on her desk, no coffee cups or water glasses. Her toy llama was shoved into the corner of the desk, almost as if someone had pushed it out of the way. The last time he'd walked past her desk he'd noticed a notepad covered with her dainty cursive.

Numbers, little bits of code and a few doodles. But it was nowhere to be seen.

Checking to make sure Joan wasn't watching, he ducked into Quinn's pod and opened the drawers in her desk. It was virtually empty, save for a few loose paper clips, a couple of pens and a pad of rainbow sticky notes.

He closed the drawers quietly and made his way over to Joan's office just as she walked out.

"I thought you were right behind me," she said, laughing. "I was talking to myself like a big old doofus assuming you were right there."

"Sorry, I got distracted."

"Never mind." She thrust a stack of papers into his hands. "This is the report. All the cards that have been activated and deactivated are listed on the first page. Then the last month's usage report is behind that. It's long, though. We have a lot of comings and goings 'round here."

"That's fine. I have an eagle eye."

Her lips formed a tight smile and she nodded. "I'm sure it serves you well. Now, if you'll excuse me, I have to go and offer someone a job."

"That must be the best part of your day."

She shrugged, the smile slipping from her lips. "Another one of Walt's nephews mooching off him and taking away jobs from people who deserve them. There's no joy in supporting that." The minute the words slipped out she blinked and waved her hand. "Oh, don't mind me. I'm a grouchy old lady. Please don't say anything to Walt."

"I didn't hear a thing." Aiden tapped his free hand against his leg as he walked back toward the meeting room, his mind whirling.

There was an important piece of the puzzle missing, and it wasn't just the name of the person leaking information. He had a feeling that everything was laid out in front of him; all he had to do was figure out how it fit together.

14

IT WAS SEVEN O'CLOCK before Aiden realized that the office had cleared out. He'd been poring over the reports Joan had given him for hours, trying to figure out if someone had accessed the building to get information.

So far, nada.

The access cards also activated the printing and scanning machines, and every item was logged with a time stamp. All emails to external addresses were run through a filter to catch any sensitive information leaving the company. And no laptops, tablets or mobile devices had been reported stolen for months.

He had access to piles and piles of data, but none of it pointed to a leak.

It was possible the informant had passed the information on via a call from a personal cell, or perhaps they'd taken a photo of the document with their phone. But trying to find evidence of that would be like trying to find the proverbial needle in a haystack.

He couldn't fail at his first assignment. There *had* to be a clue somewhere, and if the "how" wasn't presenting itself, then he'd have to dig deeper into the "who" and "why."

Motivation. That was where people always tripped up. It was easier to cover a paper trail than it was to hide intention…at least in his experience. The simplest reason for leaking information would be for financial gain. Perhaps someone was paying an employee for each bit of data that left the company.

But in his gut he knew that wasn't it. There was something more going on here.

That suspicion had only been confirmed when he'd interviewed Christopher again earlier in the day. The guy had sweated a bucket, and Aiden was positive he was hiding something.

Tapping at the keys on his laptop, he pulled up LinkedIn. Christopher's profile was sparse, and his picture looked like it had come from a wedding where he'd cropped out the person standing next to him. He had only fifty-seven connections. Aiden clicked on the list. One name jumped out at him like a jack in the box.

Alana Peterson.

Aiden switched over to Alana's profile. Quinn's friend had over five hundred connections, most of them female, from what he could tell. Looking at her job history, he couldn't see how she would know Christopher specifically, but then again, they were both in the technology industry. Maybe it was nothing.

"Doesn't feel like nothing," he muttered to himself. He drummed his fingers against the desk.

Instinct told him that Alana was connected to this whole thing somehow. He'd had a niggling suspicion about it that first night at the cocktail party before he'd started with Cobalt & Dane.

But he had nothing solid that connected her to the leak. And he'd been *positive* that Quinn was telling the truth about Alana's reason for being angry with Third Planet Studios. So what did her beef about their lack of female protagonists have to do with the information about the game design engine? The two things seemed completely separate.

"What is your deal, Alana?"

He continued to scroll through her connections until another name jumped out at him. Sarah Newell.

One click confirmed that Sarah had worked at Third Planet Studios for eleven months and hadn't taken a job since. She'd listed one freelance job for Alana's website and Alana had written her a glowing recommendation for her LinkedIn profile.

Aiden checked Alana's website and quickly found two articles detailing exclusive information on the design plans Christopher had been caught sending to his home email address. Two weeks apart, but the articles must have been small enough that no one at Third Planet Studios had picked up the connection.

He needed to find Quinn—if she knew anything at all he wanted to give her the chance to come out with it before he took this information to Rhys. He'd be pissed if she was keeping information about the case from him, but he owed her the benefit of the doubt.

Snapping shut the lid of his laptop, he packed up his things and slung his satchel over one shoulder. Hopefully, he could get her to trust him.

She's got too much baggage. His brother's voice circled around in his head. *She'll complicate your life.*

And what if she spilled the beans to everyone else at Cobalt & Dane about his connection to Logan? He'd lose their respect before he'd even had a go at building his own reputation. Then what? He could hardly go crawling back to his father *or* the FBI.

The sound of his footsteps echoed around the quiet office. A few workers remained. One guy chatted into a headset as he typed, and another was scribbling madly on a whiteboard.

"Quinn?" He stuck his head into her pod but no one was there.

It *was* after seven, no surprise she'd gone home. Still, that wasn't going to stop him from trying to find her. He pulled his phone from the depths of his satchel and dialed her number as he walked down the rows of desks. The "Super Mario" theme music cut through the air. He stopped dead in his tracks.

The sound pulled him back toward her desk until her voice mail cut in. *This is Quinn. Leave a message... unless you're trying to sell me something. Then don't leave a message.*

He yanked the chair out from her desk and found her backpack stashed on the ground. It was unzipped, her pink headphones trailing out of the opening as if she'd been interrupted halfway through putting her stuff away. Unease prickled up the back of his neck, the cold grip of intuition closing in around his stomach like an unrelenting fist.

It's nothing; she's probably gone to the restroom.

But she would have taken her bag with her if she was on her way out. At the very least it wouldn't be open like that...would it?

Sighing, he kneaded the hard knot of muscle in his neck. There was a logical explanation, something so simple he'd laugh at how worked up he'd gotten. How irrationally worried.

"You looking for something?" A short woman with curly red hair and thick-framed glasses stopped beside him.

"Some*one*. Have you seen Quinn?" He inclined his head toward her desk.

Two large eyes blinked at him behind the thick lenses as she scrunched her nose up for a moment. "No, I don't think I have. At least not this evening."

Damn. He scanned the open-plan office. You could see the whole floor, other than the management offices and the conference room. Even the reception area was only partially blocked. And the meeting rooms had glass walls in keeping with the "open and transparent" working environment that Walt touted.

"What about Zach?" he asked the woman, walking into the other man's pod and inspecting the empty desk.

A bag sat propped against a small set of drawers, but his laptop was still in its docking station. The screen was filled with an angry-looking character who had fire for hands and a manic, toothy grin.

"I overheard him saying something about going to the testing room a little while ago." She scrunched up her nose again, but this time she had the distinct look of someone who'd caught a whiff of something rotten.

"What's the testing room?"

"It's like a computer lab where they test the games. All the individual screens hook up to a big projector so they can troubleshoot problems as a group and show off new designs." She pointed in the direction of the elevators. "It's on the next floor up. Didn't they give you a proper tour?"

"It seems not."

"Want me to show you around?" she asked with a hopeful smile.

"I really appreciate the offer…" Shit, what was her name again?

"Natalie."

"Right, Natalie. Thank you for that, but I don't want to keep you from your work. I know Walt has high expectations of you all." He nodded and made his way toward the elevators.

He resisted the urge to run. Drawing attention to himself wasn't smart, although he stuck out like a sore thumb without even trying. People seemed to give him a wide berth here.

When he made it up to the next floor—taking the stairs two at a time because he couldn't bear to wait for the elevator—his heart was thundering in his chest. And not because of physical exertion.

A strange thing happened to him whenever he entered a dangerous situation. His senses narrowed and sharpened, though his hearing was still useless as shit in his bad ear. But the ringing seemed to stop enough that he could focus on the environment around him.

This floor had a corridor at the front. At one end, a glass door bore the logo of an accounting firm. It was locked. Another door—white, no window—simply said: Testing Lab. He tried the handle. Also locked.

A pin pad blinked at him innocuously. He hadn't been issued a key card—no matter, he'd bust the door down if he had to.

Pressing his good ear against the door, he strained to hear any sounds inside. Nothing.

Then he heard voices, but not from the Testing Lab.

In a handful of long strides, he'd made it to the door of an accounting firm that shared this level with Third Planet, when he realized there was a wheelchair-accessible restroom right next to it. The restroom's white door blended seamlessly into the walls, and the only thing that told you it was a bathroom was a small silver lock with an icon of a wheelchair above it.

"What do you want, Zach?"

That was definitely Quinn's voice; she sounded frustrated, but the high pitch told him she was scared.

He didn't have a weapon, so he'd have to go in with his bare hands and hope that the idiot wouldn't try anything risky. But if he laid so much as a pinkie on her…

Pressing gently against the door, he tested it to see if it was open. Locked. Fishing out his wallet from his back pocket, he plucked his gym card out. He'd busted down his share of doors, but he wouldn't risk spooking Zach.

Sliding the card into the small crack between the door and the frame, he jimmied it up until the lock mechanism snagged. A soft click told him he was in.

THE COLD, HARD tile of the restroom lined her back, giving Quinn the support she needed to stay upright. The space was larger than a regular restroom, probably four to five times as big and designed for wheelchairs and mobility scooters. But there was nothing she could use to defend herself here, not a toilet brush or a metal dish…nothing.

If it came down to it, their struggle would be decided by physicality. And that didn't fill her with confidence. If only she'd worn her steel-capped boots.

"Why the hell are you here?" Zach waved a fistful

of paper at her. Her notepad. "I know you're not a real employee. Didn't take much to figure out you're some little snitch."

Her heartbeat drummed in her ears like a toddler letting loose on a set of pots and pans, each beat making her ears ring. Making her head ache. Making the fear push higher up her throat.

Don't give in; don't give up. You can fight him...you will fight him.

"Didn't you hear me, *snitch*?" He took a step closer. In the already small space, claustrophobia grew like a weed inside her. "I know who you are. Did you think I wouldn't understand this gibberish?"

She winced. After she'd talked with Natalie, she'd jotted a few notes down, but she'd done it in code. Fragments. How the hell had he figured it out? How could she have been so stupid?

Just keep breathing.

"You're friends with *her*. Sarah." He spat the word out with vehemence. "Did she hire you?"

She ground her back teeth together. "No—"

"Liar!"

"What do you want, Zach?" The catch in her voice betrayed how hard she was trying to keep her shit together.

Just as he started to speak again, the door swung open behind her.

"Do we have a problem here?" Aiden stepped into the restroom, and the air seemed to thin around her.

"Yes, we have a fucking problem." Her heart thundered in her ears.

Zach turned, his hands balled into fists. "Stay out of it. This is none of your business."

"Are you okay, Quinn?" Aiden asked, letting the door close behind him.

He filled the space, towering over Zach and making it clear that he was in control.

Nodding, her lips tightened into a small bud. Hot tears pricked the backs of her eyes and she blinked rapidly, her shoulders hunching forward. As the energy drained out of her, the room started to spin.

"Seriously, you need to get the hell out of here." Zach's face was beet-red, his eyes wild as his head swung back and forth between them.

"Do you know what I need to do?" Aiden's voice was soft and low, a stark contrast to Zach's. He didn't have to yell because he had the upper hand. "I need to march you straight to your uncle so he can give you a lesson about what it means to be a man. Intimidating women does not make you powerful. It makes you a fucking coward and a disgrace to your family name."

"Oh, yeah? Take me to Walt," Zach goaded him. "See what happens."

"Walt might feel differently when we talk about who's been leaking information out of this company."

"It's not me." He folded his arms across his chest.

"You don't think I could make him believe it?"

Silence.

Aiden's crisp blue eyes were like icebergs, cold and hard and immovable. "Let's see who he trusts more. I dare you."

"Fuck you."

Aiden held the door open and stared Zach down. "Don't let it hit your ass on the way out."

Tension snapped in the air, the crackle of adrenaline

running through her veins as she watched. Waiting. Hoping that Zach would leave.

When he stormed out, the breath rushed out of her lungs and she slid down to the floor, knees tucked up against her chest. She wrapped her arms around her shins and tried to shrink into nothing. Tried to stop existing.

For a moment she feared Aiden would leave her and go after Zach. But he crouched down next to her, close enough that she knew he was near yet not too close that she felt threatened.

"Are you really okay?"

"I thought he…" She gulped air in, the dam holding her emotions inside threatening to burst. "I thought…"

"He's not going to hurt you." Despite the calm on his face, she sensed the rage toiling inside him.

"You let him go?"

"I didn't trust myself to follow him, Quinn. I couldn't be certain that I wouldn't…" He closed his eyes and hung his head. "I don't want to stoop to his level. But I'm not letting this go, believe me."

She nodded and pressed her head between her knees. Nausea swelled in her stomach, the memories of her previous brush with violence clamoring over one another to gain center stage in her mind. Flashes of her fear, her panic.

You're safe now. Nothing happened…nothing happened.

"Will you let me take you home?" he asked. "Please."

"You never say please." She wanted to lift her head but it felt so heavy, and here she was safe and warm with denial wrapped around her like a cozy blanket.

"I'm saying it now. I want to make sure you're okay."

"I said I was."

"It's for me, not for you."

She stayed in the darkness of her cocoon. "Okay."

Pause. "Can I touch you?"

This made her look up. "What?"

He held out a hand, the frown on his face deepening. It was impossible to tell what was going on behind those baby blues of his. But she knew one thing for certain: he wasn't here for him. No matter what he said.

They were a team. She hadn't felt it until now, because she'd been so busy concentrating on what she wanted out of this assignment. But he'd been there for her when she needed him most, and wasn't that the definition of partnership?

What if there was more to life than chasing success?

Her hand slipped into his, and he hoisted her as gently as possible from the ground. The hardness of his chest against her cheeks was as reassuring as the ground beneath her feet. Solid. Stable.

He held her up, both physically and metaphorically. A strange sense of calm fell over her as they stood, quietly motionless.

What they had was uncertain; it was tentative and a little scary. But she felt the importance of it way down in her gut. Something was growing between them and she wasn't ready to let it go.

Time seemed to melt away as they retrieved her backpack from her desk and got into a cab together. She didn't even remember them making it over the bridge, but soon she was wrapped up in a blanket on her couch.

The kettle hissed, and Aiden's footsteps were a comforting sound for her ears to follow. Anything to keep her mind off the memories. Tears dried up quickly, she'd discovered. But memories had a way of latching on and not letting go. Like leeches.

"What are you going to do about Zach?" she asked Aiden as he came over to her with a cup of hot chocolate in each hand. Two pink marshmallows bobbed in the dark liquid like fluffy little buoys.

"I am going to talk to Walt tomorrow and say that Zach threatened one of our consultants." He set the mugs down on the table in front of her and waited to see which one she picked. The one with the message "Keep Calm and Kill The Undead," obviously. "That can't fly."

"So that's it, no more assignment?"

"That depends on how he chooses to handle Zach." He circled his hand around her green One Up mushroom mug. "If Walt's not willing to do anything about his nephew, then I'll have to talk to Rhys about how we move forward. Did Zach threaten to hurt you?"

She tested the temperature of her hot chocolate. "He implied it."

"How did he get you into the restroom? Did he follow you in there?"

"He cornered me at my desk, said he knew who I was and if I didn't want to be exposed I'd better listen to what he had to say. He told me to meet him by the special access restroom upstairs." She gnawed on her lip. "I shouldn't have gone but I didn't want to ruin our assignment. I thought I could calm him down, talk my way out of it."

"You can't reason with people like that."

"No." Steam curled up from her mug in slowly winding tendrils.

"You should have come to me."

"I know."

Truthfully, she'd been more worried that Zach had found out about Alana's connection to Sarah. If Zach blew Quinn's cover, it wouldn't be the end of the world. But if he outed Alana's attempt at blackmail…that could do some serious damage to her friend.

And angry as she was, Quinn wouldn't let Alana be charged with a crime.

"What made you come after me?" she asked.

"A feeling. I was looking for you but I only found your backpack." He shrugged as if it was nothing, but the tight set of his lips and pinched brows told another story. "I was worried."

The marshmallows in her drink had dissolved and she fished the gooey remains out with her spoon. "Why?"

"Because…" he sighed. "I don't want anything bad to happen to you. I care about you, Quinn."

THE SECOND THE words were out of his mouth, Aiden wanted to take them back. Not because he didn't mean it, but because her deer-in-headlights look told him it was too soon. It took eons for Quinn to trust anyone, and spitting out his feelings like that was not the way to go.

Her lips formed a small O shape and then she snapped them shut again as she placed her drink on the coffee table. She had the goldfish imitation down pat.

"I'm sorry." He shook his head and put his hot chocolate back on the table beside hers. "I shouldn't—"

But the words were drowned out when her lips landed on his. In fact, her whole body landed on his. Her thighs covered his own, and her hands were in his hair, tugging and pulling. She kissed him like the world was about to end, with the fervor and frenzy of a woman possessed.

Teeth and tongues clashed as he kissed her back. His arms held her tight, and fear surged through him like liquid fire. Now that he knew she was safe he imagined what might've happened if he hadn't found her…and it made his soul ache.

Clasping her head between his hands he ground his lips against hers, eyes squeezed shut. Tremors running through him.

"Jesus, Quinn… I was so damn worried."

"It's okay." Her small hands touched his face, tracing the length of his nose and the outline of his lips. "We're okay."

His hands slipped around her waist and ran up and down her back. "I won't let anything happen to you, you know that, right?"

"I'm sorry, the princess is in another castle." Her breath skated over his skin as she mimicked the famous "Super Mario" words. "I'm not a princess and I don't want to be your damsel in distress."

"I don't think of you like that." She drew his earlobe into her mouth, and his body started to hum with pleasure. The persistent flick of her tongue sent all the blood in his body southbound. "Trust me."

"I do." She drew back and looked him square in the eye.

"Really?"

"Not completely…but a hell of a lot more than I've ever trusted any other guy."

"That's because I'm not just any other guy." He'd meant it as a bit of a joke but to his utter surprise, she nodded.

"You're different. Good different."

"Wow, a real live compliment from Miss Prickly herself," he teased. "I'm shocked."

"Don't get used to it. You saved my ass today so I'm being nice. It's a one-time-only deal. Expires at midnight."

"That's not even twenty-four hours." He glanced at his watch. "That's barely three."

"We'd better make the most of it, then." Her hips traced a slow circle over his, brushing over the hard length of his now very erect cock. God help him.

"You've had a shock, Quinn. The last thing I want is for you to wake up in the morning and regret this." He wasn't sure his ego could take it if she pushed him away, not now that he'd admitted out loud that he cared about her. "I'd rather go home and have the mother of all cold showers than pressure you."

"First, I'm not proposing sex because I feel pressured." Her lashes lowered and a faint blush fanned out across her cheeks. "That might not seem like much to you but it's a big deal for me. I spent a long time being afraid of my libido and what kind of trouble it might get me into. But with you it's different."

"How is it different?"

"Well, you let me be in charge, for one." The blush deepened. "Which I enjoy. But even if you're taking charge you never make me feel unsafe. Or like my needs come second."

"Your needs *never* come second." He pulled her closer. The heat their bodies generated could have burned the building to the ground.

"And I care about you, too," she whispered into his ear. "But don't tell anyone because you'll ruin my rep."

"It's our little secret."

"Good." Rocking back, she climbed off his lap and held a hand out to him like he'd done earlier. "Come on. Time's ticking."

"Wait." He couldn't let things progress further until everything was out in the open. Quinn's trust meant too much to him.

"What is it?" She withdrew her hand and toyed with the ends of her hair.

"I don't want there to be any lies between us." He raked a hand through his hair. "I think there's a chance Alana is involved in the leak."

The color drained from her face. "Go on."

"I found a connection between her and the intern... and Christopher. It's not much, but I have to listen to my gut on this one, Quinn." He stood and walked toward her, listing the details of what he'd found so that she had the whole picture. "Did you have any idea she might be involved?"

"I found out today," she said, her eyes trained on a spot in the distance. "In the meeting we had with Rhys, you mentioned Christopher had emailed himself the game designs for "Galactic Warrior." And I remembered Alana mentioning she'd received exclusive details about that game. I called her afterward and she confirmed Christopher had leaked the information to her. But I don't think she has anything to do with the engine. She doesn't want to make money selling corporate secrets...everything she does is about improving the gaming industry, not exploiting it."

"Were you going to tell me any of this?"

Her teeth sank into her lower lip. "I wanted to find proof first that Alana wasn't connected to the engine leak. I wasn't sure you'd believe me, and I was trying to protect my friend… I'm sorry." She reached out and slipped her hand into his, the gentle touch soothing him where her words had cut. "You don't believe she's responsible, do you?""

15

COLD FEAR CLUTCHED at Quinn's chest while he stood there, silent and still. She could only hope that Aiden believed her, that he trusted her enough to follow her lead. Intertwining her fingers with his, she squeezed his hand.

"Please, give me a little more time. I'll prove it's not her."

He closed his eyes for a moment. "You don't keep *anything* from me, not ever again."

"I promise." She willed him to look at her. "I'll tell you every single thing I do. I'll give you every teeny-tiny detail about my day and I won't spare any anything at all."

"There's no need to be a smart-ass, you know." He squeezed her hand back and tugged her into his chest.

"But it's what I do best." She reached up and grabbed his face, forcing his eyes to hers again. "Will you stay tonight?"

"Try and stop me."

He kissed her and all the tension flowed out of her

body. The relief that coursed through her was new. And terrifying.

But she knew one thing for certain: she never wanted to keep anything from Aiden ever again.

They shed their clothes in a flurry, leaving a trail from the couch to the bed. Groping along the wall, she searched for the light switch and plunged them into darkness a second later.

"Don't you want to see my ugly mug?" he asked, hands guiding her back to the bed.

"I just want to feel you." Her calves hit the mattress and she folded, dropping down and pulling him with her.

The heavy weight of him on top of her was reassuring, like a hot shower and blankets and her favorite slippers. But the moment he pressed his thigh between her legs, all she could see was white light behind her eyelids. Maybe this was what it felt like to connect with someone? To love someone?

The word stopped her dead in her tracks and she froze beneath him. Love? She didn't love Aiden. She couldn't....could she? He wasn't like the other guys who'd used her and tried to hurt her. She'd already admitted that.

And *God* did he have a way with his hands. But love?

"You just about leaped off the bed then." His breath was hot at her cheek, his lips searing a line along her jaw.

"I'm fine."

He pressed up on his hands, the bed moving as he shifted his weight. Moonlight danced along his skin, the slatted blinds making a stripy pattern across the bed. Outside, rain fell, and it pattered softly against the window.

She blinked, trying to get her eyes to adjust to the dark.

"You're in bed with me, Quinn. I don't want you to feel fine. I want you to feel fan-fucking-tastic."

There wasn't a shred of doubt in her mind that when it came to the physical, he'd make her body soar, unbound and uninhibited. But her heart...no. She wasn't ready for that.

"Then do it," she whispered.

His hand crept up the side of her body one rib at a time until he cupped her breast in his palm. The gentle brush of his thumb over her beaded nipple was enough to blank her mind to the confusion warring inside. Feel, not think. That was her motto for tonight.

"More," she demanded.

"Yes, ma'am."

He scraped his teeth along her breast, catching on her nipple before he drew it into his mouth. Yes, this is what she needed. Arching her back, she pressed into him, wrapping her legs around his waist and rubbing against him.

His tongue flicked over the swollen bud again and again, each movement shooting heat down between her legs. Her sex clenched, and a fluttering started low in her belly. The sound of rain-slicked tires rushing over asphalt mingled with his throaty growl at her breast.

She dragged her nails up his back and was rewarded with a groan. "You like that?"

"What?" His chuckle sounded in the darkness. "Having a gorgeous, sexy woman underneath me who's thrashing around like a tiger? Hell, yeah, I like it."

Feeling bold in the safety of the dark, she threaded her hands into his and pushed him down. "I'll thrash a little harder if you keep going south."

"And do what?" Each word was rough and filled with the promise of intense pleasure.

"You know what to do."

"Tell me." His tongue swiped over her hip bone and he nudged her legs apart with his shoulders. "You want this?"

The warm air of his breath hit the center of her sex and she gasped. "More than that."

A finger trailed over the curve of her hip then skated up and down the lips of her sex. "This?"

"More, Aiden." Her back arched off the bed and she wriggled in frustration.

"I'm not a mind reader." He parted her with his fingers and stopped, awaiting her instruction.

"Please."

The tip of his finger circled the entrance to her sex, pushing inside just enough to make her breath catch, but leaving her wanting so much more.

"Say it."

"I want you to make me come with your mouth." The words caused her brain to spark like metal on metal, lighting up the parts of her she'd buried long ago. The confident girl who loved sex, who knew what she wanted in bed and wasn't afraid to ask for it. She'd been that woman once and she could be her again. "Go down on me."

"With pleasure."

The sound of her cries filled the air as he lapped at her, circling her clit with his tongue and sucking at her flesh until the tremors caused her thighs to quake.

"You're so wet," he moaned as he pressed a finger inside her, curling it to rub against the sensitive spot inside. "So tight and hot and…"

The rest of his words faded into nothing as the first wave of her orgasm hit, rippling through her body like shimmering fire. Her hands clutched at the duvet, scrunching it in her fists as she pushed her hips against his face, not caring about anything but taking every last drop of pleasure.

She didn't have time to come down very far, because the second she'd stopped shuddering the sound of foil tearing cut through the air. A moment later he was buried deep inside her. There was nothing sweet and tender about their lovemaking. It was raw. Needy. Desperate.

He held her close as he slammed into her while he lost himself. He moaned incoherent pleasure sounds low in her ear, her name falling from his lips over and over. Like a chant, a prayer to some higher power.

With her legs wrapped around his waist, she dug her heels into his ass and urged him on. Sweat beaded on her skin, the scent of sex and man a toxic potion for her senses. Then they were falling together, shuddering and clinging to one another until it ended.

A powerful calm washed over her as he wrapped his arms around her and rolled them both until he was on his back. He called her name one last time as he rode his pleasure out.

With their heaving chests pressed together, she could feel how close their hearts beat. This was what connection was about, the closeness. The deep, soul-level satisfaction.

Maybe she *was* ready for more.

AIDEN WOKE AS the first beam of light pushed through the slats on Quinn's blinds. Her back was pressed against his chest, and her ass was cradled in his crotch. The sound of her breathing filled the air, deep and calm. She'd told him that she never slept through the night, but here, in his arms, she was dead to the world.

He brushed the hair away from her face and watched as her eyelids flickered. She was dreaming. And from the gentle tilt of her mouth it looked as if she was enjoying it.

Moving slowly, he extracted himself from her bed and pulled the sheet up over her. A contented sigh escaped her lips, and she shifted but didn't wake. He raked a hand through his hair and stood in the middle of her apartment, his eyes sweeping over the tiny kitchen and single couch.

He had a one-on-one performance meeting with Rhys today and he had to think about what he was going to say. He'd promised to keep Alana out of it for the time being. But he'd known doing that would make it look as though he hadn't made any progress with the assignment.

How do you get yourself into these shitty situations?

Tiptoeing around, he located his clothes and dressed with the stealth of a ninja. Quinn mumbled in her sleep and turned onto her back. A light snore broke the air as she slipped into a deeper sleep. Jesus, even her snoring was adorable.

"You're messed up, Odell," he muttered to himself. "You're supposed to be getting runs on the board, not covering up your progress."

Grabbing a piece of paper from the notepad on her bedside table, he scrounged around for a pen and scrawled her a note telling her they'd meet up later at Third Planet Studios.

He'd have to come up with something for Rhys, anything that could allow him to stall until he and Quinn could look at all the facts of the case and determine whether or not Alana was leaking information for profit or if someone else was to blame.

He closed her front door behind him with a soft click. Outside the streetlights were still on, but the first haze of morning light pushed through the clouds. He walked along the street, pulling his jacket tighter around him to ward off the early-morning chill.

The brisk fall of his footsteps broke the silence, pounding in time with the burgeoning headache at the base of his skull. Must be all those confusing thoughts he'd crammed in there like too many clothes in an overstuffed suitcase. They pressed against him, competing with one another for space. Distracting him.

"This is why relationships can't be your first priority," he mumbled. A relationship? Is that what he had with Quinn?

Last night he'd come across important information in the assignment, but instead of doing his job, he'd spent the night making love to Quinn. Making love…he *never* referred to sex like that. It was a term for relationships and sappy Hallmark movies, for people who believed in soul mates and happily-ever-afters.

But what he had with Quinn was more than just a physical connection—despite sex with her being hot enough to blow his socks off. Last night when he'd found her cornered by Zach…

Shit.

Before he could contemplate that can of worms his phone rang.

"Hello?"

"Son?" His father's voice came down the line without any of its usual hard-edged formality.

And since when did the old man call him *son*?

"Dad? What's wrong?" He glanced at his watch. "Has something happened to Mom?"

"She's fine." He paused for a long moment. "Everyone's fine. I just...can't a father call his son to talk?"

Aiden slowed as the entrance to the subway appeared up ahead. "What's going on?"

"I want to apologize." His father sighed and suddenly sounded as though a hundred years old instead of his usually energetic sixty-two.

"For...?"

"For pushing you into a new job after...the accident." The whirr of his father's coffee machine sounded in the background. "I wasn't able to deal with the fact that you could have died. So I tried to make everything normal. I figured if you were in a new job, working, that you were okay and we could forget what happened."

Aidan blinked. "You did?"

"We almost lost you." His father's voice cracked. "I pushed you into that position because you were safe behind a desk. I wanted you to be somewhere that didn't put you in the line of fire."

"You never told me you were afraid for me."

"Of course I was. You're *my* son, my flesh and blood. I was terrified." He sucked in a breath. "And then when you told me you were going to work for Logan, I thought there was a chance it might happen again."

"That why you didn't want me to leave the FBI."

He shook his head, unsure where this was all coming from. Unsure how he could have been so wrong about his father's intentions.

"I should have said something, but you know I'm horrible at expressing myself." His voice had started to return to normal, showing the good old-fashioned Odell strength. "Your mother says I'm less communicative than a cactus."

His lips twitched as he imagined his mother lecturing his father. "Why did you bring it up now?"

"You remember Daniel Mollino?"

He mentally flipped through faces and names until something stuck. Big mustache. Their next-door neighbor from years ago. "Yeah, he had three sons. His wife was the lady with the red hair who used to have lunch with Mom."

"He only has two sons now."

"Oh."

"We're going to Benjamin's funeral today." The glug-glug sound of pouring liquid rang through the phone. His father didn't drink a lot of coffee unless he was stressed. "Cancer. He was twenty-two."

He raked a hand through his hair. "Dad, I'm sorry. That's awful."

"It is. But it made me think." Pause. "It could have been me. It still could be me and… I need to be better. I need to talk. More."

"We all do." As angry as he'd been at his father for pushing him, he hadn't exactly been adamant about fixing things, either.

"Well, that's all I had to say." His father was now completely in control again. "I should go."

"Thanks, Dad. I appreciate the call."

"Goodbye…son."

Aiden disconnected the call and stood in the early-morning light, rooted to the ground. He'd never expected his father to come to him. In all the years they'd been a family, he hadn't made the first move for anyone. And when his father had given him the cold shoulder after he'd left the FBI, Aiden had assumed it was because his father didn't believe he could make his own decisions. In reality, he'd simply been a scared parent.

Would his father be proud of him now?

Proud of you going into work to lie to your boss? To delay closing a case and possibly risk more information coming out simply because someone batted their eyelashes at you?

No, his father would not be proud of that. Work had always come first, and integrity to the job was valued above all else. Indecision clawed at Aiden's insides like a beast. He wanted to do the right thing by Quinn, but she was asking him to shirk his duty.

By the time he made it to the Cobalt & Dane office, no answer had presented itself. It had been easy to make promises to Quinn in the cozy cocoon of her apartment. He would have said anything to soothe the fear and hurt she'd carried with her.

And if Zach had hurt her, he would never have forgiven himself. Seeing her huddled in that corner, trembling like a leaf, had done crazy things to his insides. It had made him forget all about the assignment, about his career and all the things he thought he cared about. That wasn't sex. That wasn't chemistry or attraction.

He loved her.

And now the only woman he'd ever loved wanted him to blow his career and lie to their boss.

16

QUINN WOKE AND stretched her arm out across the bed, her fingers searching for something. Warm flesh, an embrace. Aiden.

But the bed was cold. She sat up with a start. Given how small her apartment was, it was obvious he'd already left. Why was it that she seemed to sleep like a damned log whenever he was with her?

She swung her legs over the edge of the bed and stood, stretching her arms in the air and relishing the bone-deep ache in her limbs.

But doubts skittered across her mind, chasing away the comforting haze of sleep.

Why had he left without waking her, and where had he gone?

"You're not his keeper," she muttered to herself as she wandered over to the bathroom, psyching herself up to shower and face the day.

There were too many unknowns at the moment; too many ways that things could go bad. She'd become far more attached to Aiden than she'd planned, and now she was asking him to trust her. This whole thing with Alana was a goddamn mess.

She stepped into the bathroom and found a note taped to the mirror. Aiden's handwriting was scrawled across the page, a big A marking the bottom.

I have an early meeting with Rhys. I'll make it up to you. Maybe you can whip my ass at "Mario Kart" again tonight?

The note put a huge goofy grin on her face. Despite her reservations, Aiden made her feel things she hadn't dared hope to feel again.

But the situation with Alana and the Third Planet leak weighed on her mind. Her first priority had to be solving the mystery of who the leak actually was. Until she had that information Alana could still be considered a suspect.

The idea of anything happening to her friend made her sick to her stomach.

Have you forgotten about the fact that you asked Aiden for more time? What do you expect him to say to Rhys?

She'd put him in a shitty position, that was for sure. But it would be okay. She just had to think it all through.

Water sluiced over her body as she stepped into the shower and tipped her face up to the spray. There had to be a simple solution to this assignment, some small connection that they hadn't made.

There were too many separate elements: the game design plans, Alana's blackmail of Christopher, the leaked game design engine, Sarah the intern, Zach Levitt's ignored harassment behavior...

What did they all have in common?

She turned, letting the water run through her hair

and down her back as she reached for the shampoo. The foam slipped through her fingers as she massaged it into her head, her mind methodically working through the information she had.

Those facts did have one thing in common—they could all hurt Walt Dixon in some way. Financial, legal and reputational damage. And Sarah…her name kept popping up in connection with all the other players.

An idea struck her. What if Alana wasn't the only person trying to hurt Walt indirectly? Alana had gone another route because nothing she did seemed to encourage Walt to reprimand Zach. What if someone else had done the same?

She wrenched the taps off and shivered as the cool air hit her wet skin. Wrapping herself in a towel, she hunted for her phone and called Alana.

"Jeez, Quinn," her friend's not-so-happy greeting was cut off by a yawn. "Why are you calling so early?"

"Your friend Sarah, how did she get the job at Third Planet Studios?" Quinn put the phone on speaker and tossed it onto the bed while she dried off as quickly as possible.

"She had a connection there." Alana's sleep-heavy voice came through the tinny phone speakers.

"Who?"

"Uh…" Pause. "A relative, I believe."

Quinn grabbed a pair of Superman panties from her drawer and yanked them on. "Think, Alana. This is really important."

"I'm not sure. It could have been her aunt?"

No one at the company had the same surname as Sarah; she and Aiden would have noticed that. Hopping on one foot, she stuck her other one into the leg of her jeans. "How sure are you?"

"Kind of sure."

"Is there anything else?" Something told her this was the key to figuring out who was behind the leak.

"Actually, yes." Alana's voice perked up on the other end of the phone as Quinn pulled on a bra and sweater. "I do remember. When Sarah started she made a joke about how the person who'd gotten her the job was friends with the owner and was part of the hiring process. She said she was lucky because they didn't take on many junior programmers last year."

Joan. The HR manager. That *had* to be it.

Walt had insisted on keeping the HR manager involved in the investigation because he trusted her. She knew exactly what data Quinn and Aiden were looking at and who they were talking to. Not only that, Joan controlled the information they received so it would have been easy for her to omit details on any of the reports that Aiden had requested.

If Sarah was her niece she'd have plenty of motivation to want to hurt the company.

Quinn's gut gripped on to this new idea with iron fists. She *knew* she was right. Joan was leaking the information, and it probably wasn't for financial gain. Revenge was a far stronger motivator.

But why take it out on Walt when Zachary was the one who'd attacked her niece? Well, Walt had let him get away with it. And their company was a family one; perhaps the company was destined to be passed down to Zachary.

This was it, she was positive. Now all she had to do was find proof.

Given she'd woken up early, she made it into the Third Planet Studio offices ahead of the nine a.m. rush. But Joan was already there, the door to her office open just enough that the clickety-clack sound of acrylic nails against computer keys floated out. Bracing herself, she knocked on the door frame and poked her head in.

"Hi, Joan. I wondered if you might have a moment."

The older woman looked up sharply and reached for her mouse. "Is everything okay?"

Had she heard something about the incident? The concern in her voice tugged at Quinn's nerves.

"It's about Zachary," she said.

The HR manager's cheerful smile dissolved as she waved Quinn into the room. "What's he done now?"

Quinn shut the door behind her and took one of the two plush blue chairs in front of the desk. "We had a run-in last night. He appears to have found out that I'm working here undercover and he cornered me in the disability restroom upstairs."

"Jesus, Mary and Joseph," she muttered. "I told Walt that boy was no good. Are you okay?"

"Yeah, I'm fine. Aiden came looking for me and he scared Zach off." She picked at the frayed patch of denim over her thigh. "But something needs to be done about him. If he was so bold to target someone he knew was investigating the leak, what would he do to his colleagues?"

Joan's lips flattened into a thin slash of red. Her nails drummed a sharp beat against the desktop, each tap causing the light to catch on the foil-colored polish.

"This is not the first time, is it?" Quinn pressed.

"No, it's not." Joan paused. "We've had issues with a few female employees."

"Natalie warned me that I could become a target." Her nails scratched against the fraying denim until it gave way and her thigh poked through. "Like what happened to Sarah."

Joan's impassive mask slipped.

"She's your niece, isn't she?"

"She is." There wasn't an ounce of hesitation in her voice.

"And Zachary bullied her until she left?"

Quinn's phone buzzed and when she pulled it out of her pocket, Aiden's name flashed across the screen. She tapped the cancel button.

"I told her to leave. I didn't want her to be here when I fought with Walt about it." She touched the fluffy brown curls at her temple. "Surprise, surprise, Walt didn't listen to my advice about Zach. He wanted the problem to go away quietly, and he wanted his nephew left alone."

"So that's when you started leaking information." Quinn said it as though it was just another piece of information and, to her shock, Joan didn't get upset. Instead, she sighed as though a great weight had been lifted off her shoulders.

"Yes, that's when I leaked the information."

AIDEN HAD BEEN waiting around for Rhys for over an hour now. Their meeting had been scheduled for nine but the minutes were ticking well past ten, and *still* he hadn't seen hide nor hair of his boss.

All he wanted to do was head back to Quinn's place and talk through the Alana thing. He wanted to trust her judgment—he really, *really* did—but Alana's name had been on his radar from the beginning. It was entirely possible that Quinn had rose-colored glasses where her best friend was concerned. What if Alana had convinced her to cover up evidence?

He stared at his phone. The last he'd heard from Quinn was that she was following up on a hunch, but she hadn't revealed what that hunch might be. And she hadn't taken his call. He could only hope that she hadn't decided to go back to the Third Planet offices and take Zach on herself.

"Sorry to keep you waiting," Rhys said, dropping a hand down on Aiden's shoulder. "We had an issue with the servers this morning. Logan gets a little cranky when he can't access his files. Are you still okay to meet up?"

Aiden nodded and pushed out of his chair. "Sure."

Immediately, his phone rang. Quinn. What crappy timing.

"Looks like the boardroom is occupied so we can go into my office." He motioned for Aiden to follow him. "So, how are you enjoying being an employee of Cobalt & Dane so far?"

Rhys dropped down into his chair and motioned for Aiden to take one of the two seats on the other side of his desk. A photo of him and two other guys in downhill mountain biking gear, big grins breaking through their dirt-splattered faces, hung from the wall. Other than that one personal item, his office was pretty sparse and utilitarian; pens in a Starbucks New York mug, laptop, mouse, coffee cup. That was all.

"I'd been promised that you were like a dog with a bone when it came to assignments. Logan said you were the kind of guy who would go without sleep to get the job done," Rhys said. "But I'm worried about the lack of progress with this assignment based on the update you gave me yesterday." How much could Aiden tell him without betraying Quinn's trust? Could he mention that he'd rescued Quinn from the deranged nephew of their client? That they had a suspect but hadn't yet found proof?

That he'd fallen utterly and madly in love with her?

The way Rhys was staring him down there would be no point lying; the guy was smarter than to fall for any vague answers he might give. He'd just have to hope that it would be enough. "We had an incident last night."

"An incident?"

Aiden proceeded to fill Rhys in on Zach's actions and how there had been developments in finding a connection to the leak and to the intern who'd left, strategically leaving out the information about Alana Peterson.

"Okay, I'll tell Quinn to come directly here this morning and we'll pull her undercover position. Then I'll go and have a talk with Walt Dixon personally."

"Let me handle it." Aiden held up a hand. "You put me on this case and I'll see it out. But I agree that we should pull her out."

"Fine. But I want this bastard to know what his nephew is doing."

"Believe me, I'll be the first person in line to take a swing at that little shit, but Walt already knows exactly what's going on."

"Do you think it's a coincidence?"

"Uhh…" If he said yes, Rhys would think him shortsighted. If he said no, he'd want a good reason why they hadn't followed up on the connection.

Rhys interlaced his fingers at the edge of his desk. "I get the distinct impression you're leaving information out, Odell. You'd better come clean or so help me, I don't give a shit if you're Logan Dane's blood brother, you will be out of here quicker than you can say your own name."

His eyes were narrowed, his lips set into a hard line. Rhys didn't seem like the kind of guy who would blow his top very often, but right now he looked as if he was about to throw something.

"There's nothing else," he said. "We're digging into the intern and any connections she might have with the company."

"But you have nothing concrete?" Rhys raised a brow. "You've been there over two weeks and you still have nothing?"

Shit. This was exactly what he wanted to avoid.

"Are you not up to the task, Odell? I can put another consultant on this case."

"I am up to it, Rhys. I—"

"I'm not so sure you are. Around here, these small assignments should be completed quickly and quietly. The only reason we put you on this assignment was to ease you into the work here. It's a small fish." His boss shook his head. "I'm not sure how it worked when you were at the FBI, but here connections don't matter. You can't use your relationship with the boss to shield you from the work."

His blood burned a hot path through his veins. Memories kicked up from the back of his mind, taunts from his old FBI colleagues. Accusations of unfair treatment, favoritism. Nepotism.

"I will not put up with poor performance." Rhys ran a hand over the top of his closely cropped hair. "Especially not from someone who was brought in here because they're friends with the boss."

The voices screamed louder in his head. This was all going exactly the opposite of how he'd wanted it to go. Cobalt & Dane was supposed to be a fresh start…a chance for him to prove himself.

A chance to show the world what he was made of.

"I found a link between a woman named Alana Peterson and the case. I believe she may have been using one of the staff members to access inside information." The words came tumbling out, and he hated himself for going against what Quinn had asked—but his job was on the line. His reputation. His integrity.

"Okay, so when I asked you if there was anything else, you lied to me."

"No. I don't have proof, and I'm not in the habit of incriminating people before I know for sure whether or not they're guilty."

For a moment he thought the argument would continue, but Rhys tapped his pen against the edge of the desk. "Alana Peterson. Why do I recognize that name?"

Cursing under his breath, he pulled the laptop from his bag and brought up Alana's website. Right there on the "about" page was a picture of the statuesque blonde with her arm wrapped around none other than her best friend, Quinn Dellinger.

"Shit."

"What's shit?" A female voice caught both of their attention, and Aiden turned to see Quinn hovering in the door, her brows creased.

"What are you doing here?" Aiden asked, his gut clenching.

"I work here." She stepped into the office tentatively, her long pink hair hanging over one shoulder, and bounced on the balls of her colorful high-top sneakers. "And I've figured out the leak."

"Aiden told me about Alana," Rhys said, rubbing at his temples. "You should have come to me if you thought someone you knew was involved."

Quinn's eyes widened and her head swung between Aiden and Rhys. "What? No, that's not what we—"

"I'm not mad, Quinn. But we need to figure this out, and Aiden and I both agree you shouldn't go back to Third Planet."

Her fists balled up at her sides as she glared at him hard enough that Aiden thought his hair might spontaneously catch fire.

"Oh, you both agree, do you?" She planted her hands on her hips. "I'm glad you made that decision before I got here. I really *hate* having a say in what I do."

"It's for your own good." Aiden pushed up out of his chair. "After last night—"

"Last night you said you had my back," she spat.

"Why do you think I came looking for you?"

How could she doubt he had her back after what he'd done? He'd stayed with her, comforted her. Now she was angry because he wouldn't lie? She was the one who'd insisted on truth all along.

"Tell me," she said, a long breath stuttering out of her lips. "Did you have any intention of keeping your promise?"

Crap.

"Quinn." He moved to close the distance between them but she held a hand up, her entire body vibrating with anger. "Of course I did."

"I don't believe you." Her voice left no wiggle room, not an inch.

"My duty is to solve the case and follow the information wherever it leads." The buzzing in his bad ear seemed to deafen him, stuffing his head full of noise and chaos. Sucking in a slow breath, he allowed his lungs to fill and then deflate. He couldn't concentrate with that damn ringing!

You can lie to protect a life and you can lie to protect your country, but you cannot lie for personal gain.

"You wanted me to betray all my principles—"

"You've said enough." Her lip trembled but she held fast to her glare. "I get it. I'm not worth believing in."

"You know that's not what I meant."

She shook her head, sending the long pink strands of her hair scattering around her shoulders. "You lied because you wanted to get one up on me. You wanted to make sure Rhys thought *you* were the one holding this team up."

"That is *not* true."

"I guess it must be hard coming here on the graces of your friend Logan. I wouldn't want anyone to know that I got handed a job on a silver platter, either." Her voice dripped with attitude. "I prefer not to take handouts. But that's just me."

So now she was using it against him. Twisting a knife in his chest with her words, cutting him deep.

It was his worst nightmare come true. She was the same as the other FBI agents who'd resented him, who'd attributed any success he had to his father. In their eyes—and now in hers—he would never amount to anything on his own.

"I do not take fucking handouts," he said, pressing his fingers to his temples. "This wasn't about me."

It's about you. I love you.

The words danced in his mind like devils, needling him with their tiny pitchforks. Taunting him. He couldn't tell her, not while she thought so little of him.

But he'd make her understand; he had to.

"I didn't want you to do something stupid like hurting yourself by trying to shield her."

How could she not see that?

"That's just the thing, isn't it?" Her eyes narrowed into thin slits. "Where I come from, you look after your friends. You don't go behind their backs."

The air around them crackled with tension. The kind that sucked you into its vortex, chewed you up and spit you out.

"Enough!" Rhys's booming tone cut through their argument. "Quinn, I'm sorry that you feel blindsided but Aiden is right. If Alana is involved we need to investigate her. And I also don't want you doing anything stupid."

"There's no need for me to do anything stupid," she said. "It wasn't Alana who was leaking information. It was Joan." Then she walked out.

EVENTUALLY, THEY TRACKED her down, and Quinn had filled Aiden and Rhys in on the real leak. Joan Hoxton. Joan had managed to cover up her actions by doctoring the reports she gave Aiden, just as Quinn suspected. And she'd been doing it all to take revenge on Walt and Zach for their treatment of her niece. Since she hadn't profited from the information leak and Walt was reluctant to press charges, the assignment was closed. Joan quit, Third Planet Studios hired a new HR manager and Walt was finally teaching his nephew a lesson by forcing him to attend anger management classes.

Quinn would have been happier to see Zach out on his ass but at least Alana had been left out of the whole ordeal. She'd promised to leave Christopher alone... after one last email, of course, where she strongly urged him to come clean with his wife.

"You still with us?" Alana asked.

They were sitting on Quinn's couch a few weeks after the case had wrapped up. A huge bowl of popcorn, a block of chocolate and two gin and tonics decorated the table in front of them, half consumed, along with two Nintendo controllers and the box for the "Mario Kart 64" cartridge.

"I can tell you're not invested in our 'Grand Prix,'" she continued. "I *never* beat you at Rainbow Road."

"It's a death trap," Quinn said, quoting their catchphrase for the notoriously difficult level. "Maybe it's the alcohol. I really shouldn't drink and drive."

"Maybe you should kill something instead. Why don't we play 'Slayer's Faith'?"

Quinn cringed at the mention of the game Aiden had talked to her about on the first night they met. He'd looked so handsome that night, all clean-cut and professional, but she preferred the real him. The guy with the messy curls, the one who'd let her tie him up and had taken his "Mario Kart" defeat with more grace than any other guy she'd ever known.

"No, not 'Slayer's Faith.'" She let her hair hang over her face, obscuring the rush of tears that pricked the back of her eyes.

"What about 'Resident Evil'? I know you love shooting those zombies." Alana put a comforting hand on her shoulder. "I'll put the cheat code in so you can have the rocket launcher straightaway."

"That's sweet." The words stuck in her throat and she tried to clear the lump there. "But I'm not really up to it."

"Now I'm sure you're sick." Alana swept Quinn's hair back, the smile fading when she caught sight of Quinn's trembling lips and watery eyes. "Hey. That's not the reaction I was hoping for."

She wasn't going to cry, damn it. She *wasn't.*

So what were those fat, wet droplets on her face, then? "I screwed up, Alana."

"Tell me." She rested her cheek against Quinn's head. "What happened?"

It all came tumbling out like pebbles skating over a cliff's edge. The assignment, sleeping with Aiden, him saving her from Zach…her desire to be the old Quinn. The fearless girl who did what she wanted, who wasn't afraid to trust, who didn't keep things from the people she loved.

Loved…don't you mean love? Present tense.

Damn it, she did love him. What perfect fucking timing.

Realizing that she loved Aiden had come a little late, considering she'd seen neither hide nor hair of him in the past few weeks. He'd taken himself off the Third Planet Studios case after their argument and had been assigned to some top-secret project for Logan.

Meanwhile, Quinn had got all the credit for figuring out the leak. She officially started in her new capacity as Junior Security Consultant on Monday. But the victory felt hollow without Aiden by her side.

"Time for some real talk," Alana said, her fair brows crinkled. "You need to hash it out with him."

Quinn exhaled and shook her hands, trying to free herself of the nervous energy coursing through her veins. "And say what? Sorry I got a bit psycho. Sorry I pretty much said you didn't deserve your job. Sorry that you got me out of trouble and I threw it back in your face?"

"Any of those would probably be a start." Alana's lips quirked up into a smile. "Why do you think you got so upset?"

She rubbed at her eyes and sighed. "I thought we had something. It felt like more than…you know."

"You can say the word. It doesn't have to be a big scary thing anymore."

"It was more than sex." Quinn drew her knees up to her chest and wrapped her arms around her legs. "We were partners at work. And I thought we were partners outside work, too…which is silly, because we never talked about it."

"It's not silly. Sometimes you know in here." Alana tapped her chest with her finger. "You know if it feels right and if there's something there worth pursuing."

"There was," she whispered. "I felt safe around him. But I pushed him away at every little hurdle."

"Why?"

"I was scared he'd turn out like…" Ugh, she couldn't even say her ex's name. "What if I trusted him and he did something terrible to me? I'd be the fool again. Poor little Quinn Dellinger who can't tell the wolves from the sheep."

"You don't want either of those." Alana shook her

head, tendrils of blond hair escaping her ponytail. "Wolves are mean and sheep are boring."

"What do I need then?"

"A real guy. Not an ideal or a stereotype or projection of your ex…just a decent, caring guy who'll accept you as you are."

"He is a real guy." Her teeth scraped along her bottom lip. "And I think he did accept me, which is crazy, considering how screwed up I am."

"You're not screwed up, Quinn. You had a bad experience, it scared you and it takes you a while to trust. There's nothing wrong with that." Alana's hand ran over her hair. "If he really cares about you then he'll welcome the chance to talk it over."

"He won't hate me?" God, she sounded utterly pathetic. But the chance that Aiden might be willing to forgive her was a hope she couldn't let go.

She loved him and she needed him to know it…even if there was a strong chance he'd reject her.

"I really doubt it, but be prepared that he might not be ready. You might have to give him time."

She nodded. "I will."

17

STEALTH WASN'T A skill that came easily to Aiden. He was a big guy, always had been. It had taken him a while to learn how to make his footsteps fall as lightly as snowflakes, to be slow and steady and still when the situation called for it. Before his accident, his hearing had been so finely tuned he could pinpoint the smallest sound, as minute as vibrations in the air.

These days the persistent buzzing in his ear stopped him from doing that. But his other skills remained sharp.

And today he needed them.

It was a Friday afternoon and, from his vantage point behind Logan's assistant's desk, Aiden watched as the last remaining Cobalt & Dane staff left the building. Twice now someone had tried to convince him to leave for the day—Jin had tempted him with drinks at a local bar, and Logan had offered dinner at Gustoso. But nothing would deter him from this mission.

As the voices faded, he snuck out from behind the desk and darted into the IT area. Quinn's desk stood out to him immediately. She wasn't a support officer anymore but she hadn't changed desks yet. The funny memes she'd printed out were still hung from a wire, held in place with plastic superhero pegs.

He'd wanted so badly to congratulate her on the promotion but he figured direct contact might be too much.

The day she'd walked out of Rhys's office after fighting with him had been a new low point in his life. But he'd made a commitment then and there not to repeat the mistake he'd made with his father—he wasn't going to allow Quinn's walls to keep him out. He'd scale them, vault over them or take them down brick by stubborn brick if he had to. And he wasn't going to let his own hang-ups prevent him from getting close to someone.

He'd been so concerned about doing his duty he'd undermined his partner. And while he'd been trying to prove himself, Quinn had solved the case. She'd had her focus on the right thing while he had not. It'd been a difficult lesson, one that had showed Aiden what really mattered.

But all good plans of attack started with planning—and the right initial contact.

He held the small bamboo plant in his hands. The lady at the flower shop had raised a brow when he'd picked the skinny little thing from among the much showier boxes of roses and irises. But the plant had reminded him of her—unconventional, hardy and without any fanfare.

"What are you doing?"

At the sound of her voice he cursed and turned around. "I thought you'd finished up for the week."

Quinn hovered a few feet away. Her hair was braided in some intricate design that made her look like a Hunger Games extra. She wore a pair of shredded black jeans, black high heels boots and her leather jacket. Sexy ninja, indeed.

"I forgot my phone charger." Her eyes darted to the bamboo plant. "Is that for me?"

"I figured a plant brought us together the first time, maybe it would work again." He held it out to her.

She came close enough to take the plant, her fingertip tracing the length of the stem. "Does she have a name?"

"He," Aiden corrected, the pressure in his chest expanding as he tried to read her. "Leafino."

A smile tugged at the corner of her lip but her eyes remained trained on her gift. "It suits him."

"It was meant to be a surprise." Suddenly, Aiden had no idea what to do with his hands, so he shoved them into his pockets. Nervous energy flowed through his veins and he bounced on the balls of his feet. "And a congratulations for your promotion."

"You heard?" She looked up, her face glowing.

"Of course I did. I'm really proud of you, Quinn. You deserve it."

The hum of the building's air-conditioning filled the pause in their conversation, and the lights lowered to their energy-saving mode. It made the space feel intimate, personal. He wanted to sweep her up in his arms and promise her he'd never let go. Promise her he'd make up for being such a dick and not trusting her.

"I didn't do it all on my own and you know it." She hugged the plant close to her chest. "We were a team."

"And I was barking up the wrong tree." He sucked in a breath, filling his lungs to bursting before letting it all whoosh out and hopefully take some of his nerves with it. "I shouldn't have told Rhys about Alana the way I did."

She shook her head. "I'm sorry I threw it back in your face. That was a nasty thing to do."

"I deserved it."

"No." She blinked up at him. "You didn't. The thing is, I hold people to these impossibly high standards as a means of distancing myself from them. I look for people to fail because it proves that I can't trust them...and that's not fair. To anyone."

"But I knew you had a hard time trusting people and I screwed up." He raked a hand through his hair. "I regret that so much."

Before he even realized she'd moved, the bamboo plant was on her desk and she had a hand on his arm. "Is that all you regret?"

"I regret not telling you this sooner, Quinn." As gently and slowly as he could, he smoothed his hands over her shoulders and up the back of her neck, cupping her head. "You said you were sick of being scared, but the truth is I'm sick of being scared, too."

"Scared of what?" The words came out as a breath, soft. Almost imperceptible.

"I'm sick of being afraid of what other people think. I spent my whole life trying so hard to prove myself that I forgot what was important." His thumb traced the shell of her ear, feeling the bump of each of her five earrings. "Proving myself to *me*. You made me see that, Quinn. The way you're always yourself no matter what. I love that about you."

"You do?" Her eyes glimmered in the low light of the office, the clear stone in her nose winking at him as she turned her head.

"Yes. I love how you stand by your code, how you stick up for the things and the people you believe in." His lips grazed her forehead. "I guess I just love…you."

Her breath stuttered in and out as she processed what he'd said. "How can you love me?"

"You're kind of fascinating, remember?"

"And kind of sexy?" She laughed and the gravelly sound lit him up from within.

"No, not kind of. You're totally, unbelievably, *unimaginably* sexy."

Her fists clutched at his shirt, her body pressing tight against his. "Well, I have something to tell you, Mr. FBI." Even in the dark he could see the blush spread out across her cheeks. "You make me want to trust again. You make me want to have every kind of wild, crazy sex there is. You make me want to stop being afraid."

"Anything else?" His lungs felt like they might burst as he held his breath, waiting. Hoping.

"You make me want to love," she whispered. "And I do. I love you, Aiden. I want us to be a big, happy family…you, me and Leafino."

He brought his lips down to hers and all the love he felt flowed from him to her. His hands gripped her tightly, unwilling and unable to let her go. Their tongues clashed, lips and teeth joining the passionate battle as they kissed.

She shoved him hard against her desk and pressed her hips against his, eliciting a moan from deep within him. He reached behind her and filled his palms with her perky ass. Kissing Quinn could satisfy him forever, and he knew, deep down, they would love each other like this for the rest of their lives. Passionately. In totality.

"Does this mean you'll let me win at 'Mario Kart' once in a while?" he asked with a grin as they came up for air.

"Not a chance, buddy." She wound her arms around his neck and nipped at his chin. "Prepare to eat shell."

* * * * *

REQUEST YOUR FREE BOOKS!
2 FREE NOVELS PLUS 2 FREE GIFTS!

H HARLEQUIN®

Desire

ALWAYS POWERFUL, PASSIONATE AND PROVOCATIVE

YES! Please send me 2 FREE Harlequin® Desire novels and my 2 FREE gifts (gifts are worth about $10). After receiving them, if I don't wish to receive any more books, I can return the shipping statement marked "cancel." If I don't cancel, I will receive 6 brand-new novels every month and be billed just $4.55 per book in the U.S. or $5.24 per book in Canada. That's a savings of at least 13% off the cover price! It's quite a bargain! Shipping and handling is just 50¢ per book in the U.S. and 75¢ per book in Canada.* I understand that accepting the 2 free books and gifts places me under no obligation to buy anything. I can always return a shipment and cancel at any time. Even if I never buy another book, the two free books and gifts are mine to keep forever.

225/326 HDN GH2P

Name _____ (PLEASE PRINT) _____

Address _____ Apt. # _____

City _____ State/Prov. _____ Zip/Postal Code _____

Signature (if under 18, a parent or guardian must sign) _____

Mail to the **Reader Service:**

IN U.S.A.: P.O. Box 1867, Buffalo, NY 14240-1867
IN CANADA: P.O. Box 609, Fort Erie, Ontario L2A 5X3

Want to try two free books from another line?
Call 1-800-873-8635 or visit www.ReaderService.com.

* Terms and prices subject to change without notice. Prices do not include applicable taxes. Sales tax applicable in N.Y. Canadian residents will be charged applicable taxes. Offer not valid in Quebec. This offer is limited to one order per household. Not valid for current subscribers to Harlequin Desire books. All orders subject to credit approval. Credit or debit balances in a customer's account(s) may be offset by any other outstanding balance owed by or to the customer. Please allow 4 to 6 weeks for delivery. Offer available while quantities last.

Your Privacy—The Reader Service is committed to protecting your privacy. Our Privacy Policy is available online at www.ReaderService.com or upon request from the Reader Service.

We make a portion of our mailing list available to reputable third parties that offer products we believe may interest you. If you prefer that we not exchange your name with third parties, or if you wish to clarify or modify your communication preferences, please visit us at www.ReaderService.com/consumerschoice or write to us at Reader Service Preference Service, P.O. Box 9062, Buffalo, NY 14240-9062. Include your complete name and address.

HDI5

"Can you be married without having sex?"

Levi Brandon's SEAL team leader, Gray Jackson, slapped him on the back, harder than was strictly necessary. "Last time I checked, you weren't married, planning on getting married or even dating the same woman for consecutive nights. The better question is... can you go without having sex?"

He'd tried dating when he was younger. Hell. The word *younger* made him feel like Methuselah, but the feeling wasn't inaccurate. Courtesy of Uncle Sam, he'd seen plenty and done more. The civilian women he'd dated once upon a time didn't understand what his job entailed.

He certainly had no plans for celibacy. On the other hand, fate had just slapped him with the moral equivalent of a chastity belt. Levi pulled the marriage certificate out of a pocket of his flight suit and waved it at his team.

Sam unfolded the paper, read it over and whistled. "You're married?"

"Not on purpose," Levi admitted with a scowl.

HBEXP0416

Mason held out a hand for the certificate. "When did this happen?"

"I'm blaming you." Mason was a big bear of a SEAL, a damned good sniper and the second member of their unit to find *true love* when they'd been undercover on Fantasy Island three months ago. "Your girl asked Ashley and me to be the stand-in bride and groom for a beach ceremony. She didn't tell us we were getting married for real."

Mason grinned. "Heads up. Every photo shoot with that woman is an adventure."

"Yeah," he grumbled, "but can you really imagine me married? To *Ashley*?"

Ashley Dixon had been a DEA tagalong on their past two missions. As far as he could tell, she disliked everything about him—she'd been happy to detail her opinions loudly and at length. Naturally he'd given her plenty of shit while they'd been in their field together, and she'd *really* hated him calling her Mrs. Brandon after they'd played bride and groom for Mason's girl.

After they'd parted ways on Fantasy Island, he hadn't thought of her once. Okay. He'd thought of her once. Maybe twice. She was gorgeous, they had a little history together and he wasn't dead yet, although he was fairly certain he *would* be if he pursued her. But how the hell had he ended up married to her?

Don't miss DARING HER SEAL
by New York Times *bestselling author Anne Marsh,*
available May 2016 wherever
Harlequin® Blaze® books and ebooks are sold.

www.Harlequin.com

HBEXP0416

Reading Has Its Rewards

Earn **FREE BOOKS!**

Register at **Harlequin My Rewards** and submit your Harlequin purchases from wherever you shop to earn points for free books and other exclusive rewards.

Plus submit your purchases from now till May 30th for a chance to win a $500 Visa Card*.

Visit **HarlequinMyRewards.com** today

MYR16R1

Looking for more passionate reads?
Collect these stories from
Harlequin Presents and Harlequin Desire!